Evaristo Carriego

BY JORGE LUIS BORGES

Ficciones

Labyrinths

Dreamtigers

Other Inquisitions 1937-1952

A Personal Anthology

The Book of Imaginary Beings

The Aleph and Other Stories 1933-1969

Doctor Brodie's Report

Selected Poems 1923-1967

A Universal History of Infamy

In Praise of Darkness

Chronicles of Bustos Domecq

The Gold of the Tigers

The Book of Sand

Six Problems for Don Isidro Parodi

JORGE LUIS BORGES

Evaristo Carriego

A Book About Old-time Buenos Aires

Translated, with an Introduction and Notes, by
NORMAN THOMAS DI GIOVANNI
with the assistance of Susan Ashe

E. P. DUTTON, INC. | NEW YORK

Parts of this book first appeared in the following periodicals:
  Bennington Review: "Preface to the First Edition," "Palermo, Buenos Aires,"
"A Life of Evaristo Carriego"
  The American Poetry Review: "Inscriptions on Wagons"
  The Antioch Review: "Carriego and His Awareness of the City's Outskirts,"
"Foreword to an Edition of the Complete Poems of Evaristo Carriego,"
"Foreword to an Edition of the Selected Poems of Evaristo Carriego" (under the
title "Three Views of Evaristo Carriego")
  The New Republic: "Stories of Horsemen"
  The New Yorker: "The Dagger," "The Challenge" (the chapter from "A His-
tory of the Tango" here titled "The Cult of Courage")
  Translation: "Truco"
  "Stories of Horsemen" has also been broadcast by the BBC, Radio 3.
  The Introduction, under the title "On Evaristo Carriego," first appeared in
an extended form in *Bennington Review.*

Published in the United States, 1984, by
E. P. Dutton, Inc., 2 Park Avenue, New York, N.Y. 10016

Library of Congress Cataloging in Publication Data
Borges, Jorge Luis
Evaristo Carriego: a book about old-time Buenos Aires.
Includes bibliographical references and notes.
1. Carriego, Evaristo, 1883–1912—Criticism and interpretation.
2. Buenos Aires (Argentina)—Socal life and customs. I. Title.
PQ7797.C285Z613 1983   861   83-1605

ISBN: 0-525-24164-7 cl; 0-525-48085-4 pa

Published simultaneously in Canada by
Fitzhenry & Whiteside Limited, Toronto.

10 9 8 7 6 5 4 3 2 1
First Edition

To L.E.,
who justifies the world*

. . . a mode of truth; not of truth
central and coherent, but of truth
angular and splintered.

—DE QUINCEY, *Collected Writings*, XI, 68*

Contents

Introduction

I

Evaristo Carriego, a book conceived and written in the late twenties and first published in 1930, is the earliest volume of Jorge Luis Borges' prose that we have in English and the earliest that he still allows to remain in print in Spanish. But who was Evaristo Carriego? He was a minor Argentine poet who died at the age of twenty-nine in 1912, the man who, in Borges' words, "discovered the literary possibilities of the ragged and run-down outskirts of [Buenos Aires]— the Palermo of my boyhood." The reader, however, should not be too concerned about this. *Evaristo Carriego* (1930) is not very much about Evaristo Carriego (1883–1912); it is really about Borges himself and about old-time Buenos Aires. As such, it has the capacity to illuminate whole regions of the landscape of Borges' subsequent writing as well as to provide startling insights into his later attitudes and ironic statements about the writing—most of it suppressed—that preceded *Evaristo Carriego*. This book is essential to any reader already familiar with the major stories and essays, essential to anyone who wants to see painted in another corner of the still incomplete but masterly canvas of Borges' whole work.

II

When *Evaristo Carriego* appeared, it was Borges' seventh published book. Three poetry collections (gathering eighty-four poems) and three volumes of essays (gathering sixty-eight pieces) had come before—all in a truly prolific seven-year span that is still more remarkable when we consider that numerous other pieces contributed to magazines and newspapers of the time were left uncollected. In his 1970 memoir, the "Autobiographical Essay" that Borges wrote for *The Aleph and Other Stories*, he dismisses the three prose volumes as "reckless compilations" and goes on to say that

> In 1929, that third book of essays won the Second Municipal Prize of three thousand pesos, which in those days was a lordly sum of money. I was, for one thing, to acquire with it a secondhand set of the Eleventh Edition of the *Encyclopaedia Britannica*. For another, I was assured a year's leisure and decided I would write a longish book on a wholly Argentine subject. My mother wanted me to write about any of three really worthwhile poets—Ascasubi, Almafuerte, or Lugones. I now wish I had. Instead, I chose to write about a nearly invisible popular poet, Evaristo Carriego.

How much of this statement is true? How much a deliberate false track—and if so, why? A recent biography of Borges, relying on memoir here rather than on first-hand investigation, leads to some flimsy judgments. In "choosing Carriego as a fit subject for a major work," the biographer writes, Borges "was quietly stressing his rebellion against family values," thereby indicating "a decision to challenge established literary values." But, so firmly launched on his career, with so much work behind him, surely Borges had long since left off rebelling against his family. The hard facts, I find, reward us with quite different and far richer conclusions.

Evaristo Carriego has two sets of roots, one visible, one invisible. The book that gained that 1929 prize was the now suppressed essays *El idioma de los argentinos*, published the previous year. On the reverse of the title page of the essay collection, the last entry in a list of other books by Borges reads, and I translate, "In progress: *A Life of Evaristo Carriego*." Clearly, then, *Evaristo Carriego* was not the result of a last-minute decision foisted on Borges by the advent of an unexpected gift.

In an essay dated January 1926, "The Extent of My Hope"—the title piece from the second of the suppressed collections of this period—Borges informs us in a flush of nationalistic fervor that a list of the truly Argentine writers of the first quarter of this century "must include the names of Evaristo Carriego, Macedonio Fernández, and Ricardo Güiraldes." As if in pursuit of this notion, the same collection contains the piece "Carriego y el sentido del arrabal" (Carriego and His Awareness of the City's Outskirts),[1] whose half-dozen pages amount to no less than a trial balloon, a rehearsal, for the

---

1. For the complete text, see Appendix I, pp. 155–59.

book-length essay of 1930. Both the shape and essence of the later book are here in embryo: an opening description of Palermo, a swipe at José Gabriel's 1921 biography of Carriego, the gist of the critical judgments. Whole passages are even lifted from the 1926 essay and used almost verbatim in the 1930 book. "Carriego y el sentido del arrabal" begins by affirming that Carriego's poems "are the soul of the Argentine soul" and ends by announcing that "This all-too-brief discourse on Carriego has another side, and I must return to the subject one day simply to praise him."

We can trace these roots back further still. In 1925, in the foreword to his second book of poems, *Luna de enfrente* (Moon Across the Way), Borges writes that in two pieces "figures the name of Evaristo Carriego, always as something of a minor deity of Palermo, for that is how I feel about him." The latter of these two poems, "Versos de catorce" (Fourteeners), titled after its fourteen-syllable lines, tells us that "I felt that Palermo's straight streets . . . spoke to me of Carriego. . . ." The reference to Carriego in the other poem, "A la calle Serrano," is slight, but because the link with him here lies in the whole poem it is more significant. As this poem was never reprinted in any Borges collection after its appearance in the 300-copy first edition of *Luna de enfrente*, it is very little known.[2] Calle Serrano is the name of the street in Palermo on which the Borges family had once lived. "Calle Serrano," it begins, "you are no longer the same as at the time of the Centenary"—that is to say, no longer as it was fif-

---

2. I am not unaware that it was included in a 1926 anthology of vanguard verse.

teen years earlier, in 1910, when Borges had lived there as a boy and Evaristo Carriego "never missed a Sunday at our house on his return from the race-track." In the poems left by Carriego after his death is one called "El camino de nuestra casa," which loosely translates as "On Our Street," which is exactly the sense of Borges' title. The subject and the elegiac tone of the two pieces are identical. "You are as familiar to us as a thing that once was ours and ours alone," runs Carriego's poem in the rather lovely lines that Borges later singled out in his book on Carriego. The holograph page reproduced in the first edition of *Evaristo Carriego*, it may be worth noting, is from this particular poem.

The invisible roots of Borges' book on Carriego are biographical. Carriego, as well as having been a neighbor, had been a friend of Borges' father. As a boy, Borges had listened to the poet recite from memory the 150-odd stanzas of Almafuerte's "Misionero." Carriego had written prophetically, in verse, of the ten-year-old Borges in his mother's album; an inscribed copy of Carriego's poems had accompanied the Borges family to Europe in 1914; and Borges, as he tells us in his "Autobiographical Essay," read and reread them in Geneva.

There is abundant evidence, then, that Borges had been under the spell of Carriego for years. When Borges began the Carriego book he was very nearly Carriego's age at the time of his death. Both had been over the same ground with first books of verse about Buenos Aires—not the center of the city but its shabby outlying areas, principally the Palermo, where each had lived. Borges' identification with Carriego was close, and the act of writing a book about him was an acknowledgment of this connection. "Truly I loved the man, on this side idolatry, as much as any." That is Ben Jonson on Shakespeare, borrowed and condensed by Jorge Luis Borges; that is the last sentence and paragraph of Borges' 1930 book on Carriego. Nowhere else in the works of the reticent, reserved Borges—not even in his love poems—are such strong sentiments to be found.[3] Borges did not write *Evaristo Carriego* by chance or whim, nor as an act of rebellion; he wrote the book out of inner necessity.

III

Evaristo Carriego was written with compelling honesty, too, a second reason why it cannot be lightly dismissed as a failure—as it has been, on grounds that it is neither good biography nor good criticism. In common with all Borges books, *Evaristo Carriego* is highly personal and even idiosyncratic. As such, it must be judged on its own very clearly stated terms. It is not and never set out to be a conventional biography.

In the 1926 "trial" essay, Borges takes a polemical stance when he claims that "in José Gabriel's mythifying there is a pusillanimous and almost effeminate Carriego who is certainly not the man with the stinging tongue and the endless talker that I knew in my boyhood. . . ." This position is taken up again, obliquely and subtly, in the 1930 essay, in whose second chapter we read:

The events of [Carriego's] life, while infinite and in-

---

3. In his "Autobiographical Essay," Borges used these same words by Ben Jonson to sum up his feelings about Macedonio Fernández.

calculable, are outwardly easy to record, and in his book of 1921 Gabriel has helpfully listed them. Here we learn that Evaristo Carriego was born on May 7, 1883, that he completed three years of high school, that he worked on the editorial staff of *La Protesta*, that he died on October 13, 1912, and other detailed and unvisual information with which the author's disjointed work—which should be to make such information visual—liberally burdens the reader. I believe that a chronological account is inappropriate to Carriego, a man whose life was made up of walks and conversations. To reduce him to a list, to trace the order of his days, seems to me impossible; far better seek his eternity, his patterns. Only a timeless description . . . can bring him back to us.[4]

It would have been pointless for Borges in 1930 to have gone over the same ground as Gabriel in 1921.

---

4. In 1970, over forty years after these words were written, I was to learn how strongly Borges felt that a chronological account of his own life, one also made up of walks and conversations, was inappropriate or at least unsatisfying to him. Despite the acclaim that poured in from all sides following the publication of the "Autobiographical Essay" (called "Autobiographical Notes") as a *New Yorker* Profile, Borges balked at the last moment and would not allow it to be translated into Spanish and published in *La Nación,* although we had already arranged for its appearance there. Privately Borges confessed to me his misgivings about the piece, complaining that there were too many dates in it. The structuring of the essay, its straightforward chronological form, and the researching of dates had been part of my special contribution to the writing of the work. Borges' recent biographer, who thought highly enough of the piece to quote it whole and make his book a gloss on it, remarks that it was composed for an Argentine audience. On the contrary, it was conceived and written with the English-speaking reader in mind. I had wanted it to serve as a kind of introduction to Borges, in his own inimitable words, that would also serve as a frame for his writing at a time when more and more of it was being published in the United States and England. To achieve these ends, I felt—and still feel—that the essay had to be rooted in, and not outside, time.

To be of value, another book on Carriego had to be different from, even a reaction *against,* the previous one. If José Gabriel's book could have all of the facts and none of the essence of Carriego, Borges would deliberately set out to write a book that, near enough, contained none of the facts and all of the essence. That second chapter, if I have managed to count correctly, provides us with seven dates. The first of these I supplied myself in the interests of the translation.[5] Of the rest, two tell us the years certain books appeared (they are not important); two, the years certain events took place (one of them is quite incidental); and two—the years Carriego was born and died—were, as we have just seen, supplied by Gabriel. We have a man's whole life, then, with but a single vital date furnished us by his biographer. While this may appear nothing short of outrageous, I find it intriguing in its metaphysical implications, which, succinctly, are that

> These patterns in Carriego's life that I have described will, I know, bring him closer to us. They repeat him over and over in us, as if Carriego went on living in our lives, as if for a few seconds each one of us were Carriego. I believe that this is literally the case, and that these fleeting moments of becoming him (not of mirroring him), which annihilate the supposed flow of time, are proof of eternity.

Does the book light up the eternity of Carriego?

---

5. See p. 52. Fifty-two years after the publication of *Evaristo Carriego,* it makes better editorial sense to provide the date of the issue of *Nosotros* instead of its whole number, which Borges gave when, closer to that date, the reader did not require the orientation. I have done this in the opening of Chapter I as well.

That becomes less a question of the details of the physical life than a critical examination of the creative life. In this respect, Borges' judgments are basically sound, and they are also quite simple: Carriego wrote a handful of good poems, which are not the sentimental ones that have secured his popular fame. What is faulty in the criticism—in Chapter III, at least—is the perfunctory and limited nature of much of the analysis. Having chosen to discuss a certain set of poems, Borges quite soon falls into ticking off a list, of dealing with the pieces by rote. But once he abandons this rigid scheme and ranges more widely and deeply, as he does in Chapter IV, his comment comes alive again and we are amply rewarded. In the "Autobiographical Essay" he admits that "The more I wrote the less I cared about my hero" and also that "I became more and more interested in old-time Buenos Aires." If we emend this to read "my hero's poems," there is an element of truth in it. From internal evidence I suspect that the strong opening chapter, on Palermo, was written last, after the biographical and critical sections had begun to pall and still had not yielded up pages enough to fill out a whole volume.

At any rate, the remark about his hero's fate gives a nice insight into why Borges never wrote a novel and a truer reason than his frequently repeated, self-deprecating claim of sheer laziness. Borges was simply never able to sustain interest in a single person or set of persons for the span of time and space a novel requires. One has only to examine the pieces in *A Universal History of Infamy* to see this, or his perfect outline for a novel, the seven-page story called "The Dead Man." Any man's life, Borges holds in another story, "is made up essentially *of a single moment*—the moment in which [he] finds out, once and for all, who he is." That, of course, is the moment of his eternity; all the rest is mere data, or, put another way, as Borges very neatly does at the outset of *Evaristo Carriego*, "reality comes to us . . . not in the proliferation of facts but in the enduring nature of particular elements."

The difference between this book's projected title in 1928 and its final title in 1930 is telling. *Evaristo Carriego* should be taken neither as biography nor as literary criticism but as an exercise in belles lettres.

IV

It is unfortunate that by shrouding this work in mystery and belittling it Borges has paved the way for critics to misunderstand it. "Some books are to be tasted," wrote Bacon, "others to be swallowed, and some few to be chewed and digested. . . ." If the student of Borges' work chews this one, if he or she reads it with diligence and attention, there is no end to the pleasure and profit that can be derived from it.

In *Evaristo Carriego* we find a very early use of the technique of random enumeration learned from Whitman, exercised throughout Borges' work, and brought to perfection in a certain page of "The Aleph." We find the first reference to his interest in the techniques of filmmaking, a last ultraist image, the inadvertent title of a story not to be written for another four years, the growing command of his wide-ranging reading habits which intelligently, in the span of a single paragraph, clarify a point with quotations from or references to Shaw, the Gnostics, Blake, Hernández, Almafuerte, and Quevedo. On one page, speaking of Carriego's fondness for tales of blood and thunder, Borges recounts an episode concerning the death of the outlaw Juan Moreira, "who went from the ardent games of the brothel to the bullets and bayonets of the police." Immediately we recognize the germ here of the wonderful story "The Night of the Gifts," which Borges did not put on paper for forty-five or so more years. On another page we read that Carriego "never exhausted the night," and here we spot one of Borges' favorite (and sometimes abused) rhetorical devices—the hypallage, the figure of speech that reverses the order of a customary proposition, or, as Borges himself once put it, the figure in which an epithet is defined by what surrounds it (Milton's studious lamps, Lugones' arid camels). Somewhere else, in reading how, as a boy, Carriego presented himself to the local political boss of Palermo—he "told Paredes he was Evaristo Carriego, from Honduras Street"—we can hear the way, in a later sketch by Borges, one Bill Harrigan introduces himself after he has gunned down his first Mexican: "Well, I'm Billy the Kid, from New York." Or, in coming upon the words "penetrating revolvers," we recognize another hypallage, one that Borges was to repeat almost exactly three or four years later in another part of *A Universal History of Infamy.* Or we stumble on an unusual and uncharacteristic blind spot, such as the notion that Kipling was of mixed English and Indian blood. I puzzle why Borges never set this right in the book's second edition twenty-five years later, when he set one or two other matters straight. In 1937 he reviewed Kipling's autobiography, which surely made him see this error.

Evaristo Carriego also affords us an opportunity to

delve into that aspect of Borges' prose of the twenties of which he has remarked, "I was doing my best to write Latin in Spanish. . . ." If a heavy reliance on Latin syntax is a particular mark of his early prose, then the book on Carriego certainly falls into the category of early prose. A look into this Latinate Spanish will serve to illustrate one of the difficulties of translating Borges at the same time as it helps account for the uneven quality of many of his translations into English.

Take an example from Chapter II. Borges here lists a few of the elements that made up the pattern of Carriego's daily life. The first of these elements is *"los desabridos despertares caseros"*—literally, "the insipid waking ups domestic." There are no case endings here to guide us; we have only the required grammatical agreement of the two adjectives with the noun. Since "waking up" is in the plural, it obviously means waking up more than once, or waking up every morning. But *"caseros"* is trying to function as an ablative, the case used to express the relation of separation. So this becomes "at home." Roughly, then, we have "the insipid waking-up-every-morning at home." When we wake up and where overlap enough to make one of them unnecessary. Dealing next with the first adjective, *"desabridos,"* and amplifying a bit to express the plural of "waking up," we refine further and come up with "the humdrum business of waking up in the morning." Now, while I feel I have achieved accuracy here—that is, got the meaning—there are any number of ways of saying the same thing: "the pointlessness of getting up in the morning," "the daily drudgery of getting out of bed." Accuracy alone does not make a translation good, but it is the starting point of good translation. The problems presented by Latin constructions in Borges' writing baffle native Argentine readers as much as they do Borges' translators, nor are academic credentials a guarantee of unraveling or understanding exactly all that Borges writes. A knowledge of Spanish, too, is only a starting point.

V

Evaristo Carriego has had two lives. There was the modest first edition of 118 pages of text, bound in pink wrappers, that corresponds to the first seven chapters of this edition. A quarter of a century later, in 1955, came a new edition, filled out with a half-dozen miscellaneous pieces written in the early fifties (chapters VIII through XII here). For the most part, these round out the book in terms of old-time Buenos Aires and not of Carriego. Work of Borges' rich maturity, they stand in little need of elucidation.

Two of them, however, are corrective, and as such they shed light on the key problem of why Borges found it necessary to suppress so much of his early writing. The brief 1950 foreword to an edition of Carriego's poems contradicts nothing Borges wrote about Carriego in 1930; nor does the piece say anything about Carriego's poetry. Three pages long, it is set out with tremendous reserve, and its perspective is one of great distance. Obviously, Borges has refrained from a stated condemnation of the poems; one cannot very well damn the volume one has agreed to preface. The piece's brilliance is in its speculation about how Carriego became Carriego, but that brilliance resides in a display of Borges' imaginative powers and may, really, have little to do with the factual truth about Carriego. By what they do not tell us, by what they hold back, these pages mark the end of Borges' enthrallment to Carriego.

The long essay on the tango's history is another matter. A complete rewriting of a piece published early in 1927 and later collected in *El idioma de los argentinos,* its viewpoint and its conclusions are an about-face. The first essay is nationalistic to the point of xenophobia; the later work not only is universal but also berates much of the narrowmindedness of the earlier judgments. Comparison of these two pieces reveals the extent of Borges' journey through the years from callowness to wisdom.

Publicly and privately, Borges has stated that he has kept his early work out of print because it was either badly written or of little value. While indeed some of it is ephemeral and some less strikingly composed, he himself has given the lie to this claim and at the same time paid tribute to the worth of much of this early writing by having recast or otherwise reused it. What Borges is really trying to suppress is content, not form; I refer to those expressions of virulent Argentineness that now embarrass him and that he has spent the intervening years living down. This, of course, is greatly to his credit although somewhat to our loss, for, in keeping to his course, Borges has thrown out contaminated and uncontaminated matter together.

And so with Carriego. Has Borges disowned him, too, along with the unacceptable nationalism because, on looking back, the two seemed part and parcel of each other? I think he has. I also think that it is a mistake to accept Borges' dismissal of Carriego at face value and to regard it as the final word. Carriego's mark on Borges is indelible: the roots of such poems as "Empty Drawing Room," "Plainness," and many others are in Carriego; and, remarkably, a prime source for "The Aleph," written in 1945, surely lies in the Carriego sonnet "Como en los buenos tiempos."

It would be unfortunate were readers to be discouraged from reading *Evaristo Carriego* because of the samples of it they have seen elsewhere in incoherent translations. In the appendixes I have given two pieces—Borges' first and his latest statements on Carriego. Written nearly half a century apart, they fill out the picture that this book offers.

Norman Thomas di Giovanni

Swimbridge, Devon
April 3, 1982

Translator's Acknowledgments

To the Guggenheim Foundation, which made me a Fellow some years ago, when the translation of this book was first undertaken. Their generosity gave me the time to delve unhurriedly into background sources.

To my invaluable friend Adalberto Makowski, who, in St. Andrews, Scotland, provided much guidance in the original draft.

To Walter Acosta and Elena Segade, who, from Bush House, in London, cheerfully unraveled problems of River Plate slang.

To Cristina Hülskamp, who, in the unlikely setting of 9, Wilton Crescent, London, S.W.1, showed me the rudiments of the game of truco. I went to her with the pack of Spanish playing cards that Borges presented me with on my arrival in Buenos Aires back in 1968.

To Borges, of course, a constant kindly presence in both my life and my work.

Most of all to Susan Ashe, whose name appears on the title page as a mark of her inestimable contribution to this translation. She did not type the final draft (I do my own typing); she did not ransack the shelves of the London Library or of the St. Andrews University Library (I do my own investigating). She worked with me in shaping the final English text, bringing to bear on it a flair for linguistic precision and a knowledge of Latin and other languages that make the task of reading Borges' Spanish an even deeper pleasure. The formula dictates that I claim that while she provided much that is good in the translation I alone am responsible for the lapses. That would be patronizing and untrue. It is my tribute to her that I am able to say that she shares equal responsibility with me for both the good *and* the less good.

Borges would be amused and delighted to know that his book on old Buenos Aires, translated by an American working in Scotland and England, had the secret assistance—here made unsecret—of an Uruguayan Pole, various of his own countrymen and countrywomen from both *bandas* of the river, as well as an Indian-born Englishwoman. It is by now axiomatic that Borges is the most international of figures.

The translator's notes are marked with an asterisk and can be found in the Notes section at the back of the book. All numbered notes found at the bottom of the page are from the original Spanish edition.

Evaristo Carriego

Preface to the Second Edition

For years I believed I had grown up in a suburb of Buenos Aires, a suburb of dangerous streets and showy sunsets. The truth is that I grew up in a garden, behind a fence of iron palings, and in a library of endless English books. The Palermo of the knife and guitar throve (I am told) just around the corner, but those who populated my days and gave a pleasant shiver to my nights were Stevenson's blind buccaneer, dying under the horses' hooves, and the traitor who left his friend behind on the moon, and the time traveler who brought back from the future a withered flower, and the genie imprisoned for centuries in a Solomonic jar, and the Veiled Prophet of Khurasan, who hid his leprosy behind silk and precious stones.

What was going on, meanwhile, on the other side of the iron palings? What everyday lives were fulfilling their violent destinies only a few steps away from me in some unsavory saloon or ominous vacant lot? What was Palermo like then, and how beautiful would it really have been?

This book, which is less documentary than imaginative, tried to address itself to these questions.

J.L.B.

Buenos Aires
January 1955

Preface to the First Edition

Evaristo Carriego's name will, I feel sure, take its place in the *ecclesia visibilis* of Argentine letters, whose pious instruments—elocution lessons, anthologies, and histories of our literature—will include him for all time. I am also sure that he will take a place among the most true and exclusive *ecclesia invisibilis*, among the farflung congregation of the faithful, and that this more worthy membership will not owe itself to the plangent element in his work. These are the views that I have attempted to substantiate in this study.

I have also given consideration—perhaps with undue eagerness—to the daily realities that he strove to reflect. I have tried to work from facts and not conjecture. I accept the risk involved, suspecting that to mention Honduras Street and to sit back and watch the haphazard repercussions that name sets off is a less fallible method—and an easier one—than to define Honduras Street in lengthy detail. No one with an affection for Buenos Aires will grow impatient with me for my extended treatment. For that reader, I have added the chapters of the supplement.

I have made use of Gabriel's helpful book and of the studies by Melián Lafinur and Oyuela. I am also grateful to Julio Carriego, Félix Lima, Dr. Marcelino del Mazo, José Olave, Nicolás Paredes, and Vicente Rossi.

J.L.B.

Buenos Aires
1930

I.
Palermo, Buenos Aires

Confirmation of Palermo's considerable age is owed to Paul Groussac, and it is recorded in a footnote on page 360 of the fourth volume of the *Anales de la Biblioteca*. The proofs, or instruments, were published only much later, in the July 1929 issue of *Nosotros*. There we find mention of a Sicilian, one Domínguez (Domenico) de Palermo, from Italy, who added the name of his birthplace to his given name, perhaps so as to have at least one name that could not be turned into Spanish, "and he arrived in his twentieth year and entered into wedlock with a daughter of the garrison." This Domínguez Palermo, purveyor of beef to the city between the years 1605 and 1614, owned a stockyard beside the Maldonado, where wild cattle were herded and slaughtered. These herds have long since been butchered and forgotten, but specific reference comes down to us of a "dappled mule grazing in the pastures of Palermo, at the edge of this city." I see the animal ab-

surdly clear and tiny in the far reaches of time, and I
have no desire to add anything to it. Let this solitary
mule suffice. The way reality comes to us—in a
stream of flashes punctuated by ironies, surprises,
and portents as strange as surprises—can be captured only by a novel, which would be inappropriate
here. Fortunately, reality comes to us not only in this
rich way but also through memory, the essence of
which lies not in the proliferation of facts but in the
enduring nature of particular elements. This is the
innate poetry of our ignorance, and I shall seek no
other.

Within the confines of Palermo are the neat
farm and the foul slaughterhouse, and at night an
occasional Dutch smuggler would moor his craft
along the riverbank out beyond the swaying bul-
rushes. To recapture this almost static prehistory
would be to weave a meaningless chronicle of infinitely small processes: the stages of the haphazard
centuries-long encroachment of Buenos Aires upon
Palermo, which at that time was little more than an
ill-defined patch of marshy ground out in the hinter-
land. The best approach, if we were to adopt the
techniques of filmmaking, would be to present a con-
tinuous flow of vanishing images: a mule train
laden with wine casks, the less tame animals blink-
ered; a long, flat stretch of water on which a few wil-
low leaves float; a phantasmal wandering soul high
on his horse, fording flooded streams; the open
range, where absolutely nothing happens; the re-
lentless hoofprints of a herd of cattle being driven to
the Northside stockyards; a cowhand (silhouetted
against the dawn) who dismounts from his spent
horse to slit its broad throat; smoke from a fire

dispersing into the air. So it was until the arrival of Juan Manuel de Rosas,* today the legendary father of Palermo and not the mere historical one, as was Groussac's Domínguez-Domenico. Settlement by Rosas was not without effort. A villa mellowed by time out along the Barracas road was the custom of the well-to-do in those days. But Rosas wanted to build; he wanted a house of his very own, not one steeped in other people's lives or even used by them. Thousands of cartloads of loam were hauled in from "the Rosas alfalfa fields" (later known as Belgrano) to level and enrich the clayey ground, until Palermo's virgin soil and the unyielding land surrendered to his will.

Around 1840 Palermo rose to become the headquarters of the Republic, the dictator's court, and a swear word in the mouths of Unitarians. I shall not recount this period of its history, so as not to tarnish the rest. Let me only mention "a white stuccoed house called his palace" (Hudson, *Far Away and Long Ago,* page 108) and the orange groves and brick-walled pond with its iron paling, where the Restorer's boat bobbed excitedly on those voyages that were so skimpy that Schiaffino remarked that

Rowing in such shallow waters could not have afforded much pleasure, and so short a turn would have been akin to a pony ride. But Rosas sat at his ease; whenever he looked up he saw outlined against the sky the guards on duty around the fence, searching the horizon with the alert eye of a lapwing.

That court was already fraying at the edges: the

Hernández Regiment's squat cantonment of raw adobe and the brawling, bawdy hovels of the half-breed camp followers, the Palermo Garrison. The neighborhood, as is obvious, had always been a stacked deck, a two-headed coin.

That brazen Palermo lasted for twelve years, in the hurly-burly of the demanding presence of a corpulent, fair-haired man who trotted up and down the spotless paths, dressed in blue uniform trousers with a red stripe, a crimson jacket, and a broad-brimmed hat, brandishing a long cane, an airy-light scepter. From Palermo late one afternoon this dreaded man led his army in what was little more than a rout, a battle lost in advance—the battle of Caseros. Into Palermo rode another Rosas, Justo José de Urquiza, with the semblance of a wild bull and the crimson ribbon of the Mazorca around his ridiculous top hat and his magnificent general's uniform. He rode in, and, if Ascasubi's pamphleteering is not mistaken,

> en la entrada de Palermo
> ordenó poner colgados
> a dos hombres infelices,
> que después de afusilados
> los suspendió en los ombuses,
> hasta que de allí a pedazos
> se cayeron de podridos . . .

[he ordered to be hanged at the entrance of Palermo two wretched men who, after being shot, were strung from the ombus, until they rotted and fell away in pieces . . .]

40

Later, Ascasubi turns his attention to the dismissed Entre Ríos troops of the Great Army:

Entre tanto en los barriales
de Palermo amontonaos
cuasi todos sin camisa,
estaban sus Entre-rianos
(como él dice) miserables,
comiendo terneros flacos
y vendiendo las cacharpas . . .

[Meanwhile, clustered on the marshes of Palermo, shirtless almost to a man, were Urquiza's Entre Ríos troops, scum (in his words) eating lean calves and selling off their equipment . . .]

Thousands of days no longer known to memory, misty zones of time, waxed and waned, until, via a number of individual foundations—the Penitentiary, in 1877; the Northside Hospital, in 1882; the Rivadavia Hospital, in 1887—we reach the Palermo of the eve of the nineties, when the Carriego family settled there. It is this Palermo of 1889 that I wish to write about. I shall tell all I know without reservation, without a single omission, for, like transgression, life conceals itself, and we have no way of knowing what the important moments are in God's eyes. Besides, details are always poignant.[1] I shall put down everything even at the risk of recording

---

1. "[T]he pathetic, almost always, consists in the detail of little circumstances," remarks Gibbon in one of the last footnotes of Chapter 50 of his *Decline and Fall*.

facts that, though well known, will all too soon disappear through oversight, mystery's chief aspect and most distinctive feature.[2]

Among the auctioneers' flags out beyond the tracks of the branch line of the western railroad, which cut through the area known as Centro América, the neighborhood slumbered not only over virgin land but also over the bodies of small farms that were being dismembered, brutally carved into lots that were later to be trampled by saloons, wood-and-coal yards, backyards, tenements, barbershops, and stables. Here, suffocated by surrounding houses, is one of those gardens with barren palm trees among tools and implements—the run-down, mutilated relic of a great farm.

Palermo was heedless poverty itself. Fig trees cast shadows over walls; the little window balconies of ordinary people opened onto days that were all the

---

2. I maintain—and I wish neither coyly to evade nor boldly to parade paradox—that only new countries have a past; that is to say, an autobiographical memory, a living history. If time is a succession of events, we must admit that where more things are happening more time is passing, and so it is on this inconsequential side of the world that time is most profuse. The conquest and colonization of these domains—a handful of fear-ridden mud forts clinging to the coast and watching the curved horizon, the bow that shoots forth Indian raids—was so indecisive that, in 1872, one of my grandfathers was to command the last major battle against the Indians, bringing the sixteenth-century conquest to a conclusion only after the middle of the nineteenth century. Be that as it may, why resurrect the past? In Granada, in the shade of towers hundreds of years older than the fig trees, I did not feel the passage of time, but I have felt it in Buenos Aires on the corner of Pampa and Triunvirato, today an utterly featureless place of English-style roofs, three years ago a place of smoky brick kilns, and five years ago a jumble of small pastures. Time—a European sentiment of a people with a long past, and their very justification and glory—moves more boldly in the New World. Young people, in spite of themselves, sense this. Over here we are contemporary with time, we are brothers of time.

same; the forlorn notes of the peanut vendor's horn explored the twilight. Atop the humbleness of the houses it was not uncommon to see masonry urns, crowned aridly with cactus, a sinister plant which in the universal sleep of other plants seems to belong to a nightmare zone but which is really so tough, growing in the least hospitable soil and in desert air, and is vaguely regarded as ornamental. There were also happy moments: the patio grapevine, the local tough's strutting step, the rooftop balustrade with the sky showing through.

A streaked greenish horse and its Garibaldi did not always spoil the old city gates. (The malady is widespread: there is no square that does not have to put up with its bronze lout.) The Botanical Gardens, silent dockyard of trees and home of all Buenos Aires strolls, formed a corner with a shabby earth-paved square; not so the Zoological Gardens, which at the time was called "the wild beasts" and was farther north. Today (smelling of candy and tigers) it occupies the place where a hundred years earlier the Palermo Garrison teemed and brawled. Only a few streets—Serrano, Canning, Coronel— were grudgingly cobbled, and this surface was interspersed with smooth paving stones for flat-bedded wagons, impressive in procession, and for splendid open carriages. A horse-drawn streetcar, the Number 64, an obliging vehicle that shares the founding of Palermo with the all-powerful earlier ghost of Rosas, jolted its way up Godoy Cruz Street. The driver's cocked visor and milonga-playing trumpet* aroused the wonder and emulation of the whole neighborhood, but the conductor—that professional doubter of other people's honesty—was a much-attacked institution, and many a hoodlum tucked his ticket in his fly, saying indignantly that if the conductor wanted to see it, all he had to do was take it out.

I seek nobler realities. Toward the boundary with Balvanera, to the east, were a number of large rambling houses, each with a string of patios one behind the other, yellow or brown houses with entranceways in the shape of an arch—an arch repeated mirrorlike in the next entranceway—and with a fine grillwork gate. When impatient October nights brought chairs and people out onto the sidewalks and the deep houses let themselves be looked into right to the back, where yellow lights burned in the patios, the street was intimate, informal, and the hollow houses were like a row of lanterns. I can best summon up this feeling of unreality and serenity in a story, or symbol, that seems always to have been part of me. It is a fragment snatched from a tale that I once heard in a saloon and that was at the same time both trivial and involved. I reproduce it with some uncertainty. The hero of this reckless Odyssey was the classic gaucho on the run from the law, this time betrayed by a character who was a vindictive cripple but who had no equal with the guitar. The story, the bit of it I have salvaged, tells how the hero managed to escape from jail; how he was compelled to wreak his vengeance in the space of a single night; how he vainly searched for the traitor; how, as he roamed the moonlit streets, the exhausted wind brought him snatches of the guitar; how he followed this trail through the labyrinths and the shifting of the wind; how he came to the far-off doorway where the traitor was playing his guitar; how, elbowing his way through the onlookers, he lifted the cripple on his knife; how he walked away in a daze, leaving be-

44

hind, dead and silenced, both informer and telltale guitar.

On the west side of the neighborhood, Italian immigrant poverty lay exposed. The term *las orillas,* the city's outskirts, fits uncannily that bare expanse where the land takes on the indeterminateness of the sea and seems to be what Shakespeare was referring to when he said, "The earth hath bubbles, as the water has. . . ." To the west ran dirt alleys that grew progressively poorer in the direction of the setting sun. Here and there a railroad shed or a shallow pit where agave grew or an almost whispering breeze abruptly heralded the pampa. Or perhaps one of those small unplastered houses with a low grilled window—a yellow blind with a scene painted on it sometimes hung there—that, without any sign of human participation, the solitude of Buenos Aires seems to breed. Farther on was the Maldonado, a dried-out yellow ditch that stretched aimlessly from the Chacarita cemetery and that by a fearful miracle would go from a parched death to inordinate quantities of raging water, which rounded up the decaying hovels along its banks. About fifty or so years ago, beyond that uneven ditch, or death, heaven began—a heaven of whinnying and manes and lush grass, a horses' heaven, the lazy happy hunting ground of retired police horses. Toward the Maldonado the native hooligans thinned out and Calabrians took their place. Owing to their dangerously good memory for grievances and to their treacherous knife wounds delivered on long installments, they were people with whom nobody wanted to tangle. Here Palermo took on a melancholy air, for the Pacific railroad, which skirted the stream, gave off

45

that strange sadness of things large and enslaved, the gates of grade crossings as tall as the shafts of resting carts, straight embankments, and platforms. This side of Palermo ended in a border strip of chugging smoke and a shunting of clumsy freight cars. Beyond, the Maldonado widened and went on its stubborn course. It is now being imprisoned, and that almost endless lonely stretch which a short time ago was channeled underground, around the corner from the Paloma Café, where truco was played, will be replaced by an inane street of English-style roof tiles. Of the Maldonado all that will remain will be our memories of it, lofty and personal, and the best Argentine popular farce and the two tangos that bear the river's name—an early one, which, being the stream's contemporary, made no fuss about it, and was only for dancing and a chance to show off one's best tango steps; the other, a plaintive ballad-tango in the later style of the Boca—and some photograph cropped so closely that it destroys the essence, the impression of space, therefore giving the river a mistaken other life in the minds of those who never knew it.

Now that I think about it, I do not believe that the Maldonado was any different from other very poor places, but the notion of its rabble having a riotous time in lewd brothels, in the shadow of flood and doom, prevailed in the popular imagination. Thus, in the skillful farce previously mentioned, the stream is not a handy backdrop but a living presence far more important than the characters, Nava the mulatto, the half-breed Indian girl Dominga, and El Títere. (The Alsina Bridge, with the as yet unhealed wounds of its recent knife-fighting past and its memory of the great civil war of 1880, has supplanted the

Maldonado in the mythology of Buenos Aires. As to the reality, it is well known that the lowliest neighborhoods are often the most pusillanimous and that a terrified respectability flourishes in them.) From the direction of the stream high dust storms sailed in and canopied the day; from there the wind came howling off the pampa, calling at all the south-facing doors and leaving thistle flowers in the entranceways; from there came the devastating clouds of locusts that people tried to scare away with shouts;[3] from there came the solitude and the rain. That whole stretch had a taste of dust.

Toward the brown waters of the River Plate, toward the woodland, the neighborhood was harder. The first buildings in that area were the Northside slaughterhouses, which took up some eighteen square blocks between the yet-to-come Anchorena, Las Heras, Austria, and Beruti streets; today their only relic is the name La Tablada, the Stockyards, which I heard from the mouth of a wagon driver who was ignorant of the place's former use. I have led the reader to imagine a vast open area covering many blocks, and although the corrals themselves disappeared in the 1870s, that image typifies the place, which was always taken up with large properties— the cemetery, the Rivadavia Hospital, the prison, the market, the municipal cattle pens, the present-day wool-scouring sheds, the brewery, and Hale's orchards—all surrounded by the abject misery of downtrodden lives. Hale's was famous for two reasons: for its pear trees, which nearby urchins looted in furtive raids, and for the ghost that haunted the

---

3. Since these locusts carried the sign of the cross, the mark of their divine provenance, to destroy them was sacrilege.

Agüero Street side, its impossible head leaning against the crosspiece of a lamppost. For, added to the real dangers from arrogant knife-wielding hoodlums, there were the imaginary perils of popular legend; the "widow" and the outlandish "tin pig," as sordid as the riverside itself, were the most feared creatures in this local religion. Up to that time, this part of the Northside had been a rubbish dump, so it is only natural that the remains of ghosts should gather in its air. There are poor street corners in Palermo today which have not tumbled down only because they are still being propped up by dead hoodlums.

Along Chavango Street (nowadays Las Heras) the last wayside bar was La Primera Luz, First Light, a name which, in spite of suggesting the habit of rising early, gives an impression—justly so—of dark streets brimming with nobody, and finally, after a tiring slog, the human light of a saloon. Between the dusky-pink walls of the Northside cemetery and the far end of the Penitentiary there began to materialize from the dust a slumlike jumble of single-story, unplastered dwellings. Its nickname, Tierra del Fuego, was a byword. A shambles from the outset, street corners either menacing or deserted, furtive men signaling to each other in whistles and suddenly disappearing into the darkness of back alleys— all these things spelled out the nature of the place. The neighborhood was a last outpost. Petty criminals on horseback, petty criminals in soft hats pulled low over their eyes and in the kind of baggy trousers worn by gauchos, either by habit or by compulsion kept up a war of single combat with the police. The slum fighter's blade, although not as long—it was the mark of a brave man to use a short knife—was more finely tempered than government-issue sabers, since the state was likely to go in for high cost and poor quality. The short knife was wielded by an arm on the lookout for violence, one more skilled in the quick movements of a scuffle. Thanks only to its rhyme, a fragment of this verse has survived forty years of attrition:

Hágase a un lao, se lo ruego,
que soy de la Tierra'el Juego.[4]

[Move aside, please; I'm from Tierra del Fuego.]

This was not only the land of the knife fight but also the land of the guitar.

As I set down these facts retrieved from the past, I am haunted with seeming arbitrariness by that line of gratitude from "Home-Thoughts," "'Here and here did England help me. . . .'" Browning wrote it thinking about self-sacrifice on the high seas and about the tall ship, carved like a rook in a chess set, where Nelson fell. Quoted by me—along with a translation of the country's name, because for Browning the name of England had the same immediacy—it stands as a symbol of lonely nights, of long ecstatic walks through the endless neighborhoods of Buenos Aires. The city has a depth, and never once, in disappointment or grief, did I abandon myself to its streets without receiving unsought consolation either from a sense of unreality or from a guitar played in the depths of a patio or

4. A. Taullard, *Nuestro antiguo Buenos Aires,* p. 233.

from the touch of other people's lives. " 'Here and here did England help me' "—here and here did Buenos Aires come to my aid. This is one of my reasons for writing this first chapter.

II.

A Life of Evaristo Carriego

That one person should wish to arouse in another
memories relating only to a third person is an obvious paradox. To pursue this paradox freely is the
harmless intention of all biography. The fact of my
having known Carriego does not, I contend—not in
this particular case—modify the difficulty of this un-
dertaking. I have in my possession memories of
Carriego: memories of memories of other memories,
whose slightest distortions, at the very outset, may
have increased imperceptibly at each retelling. These
memories preserve, I am sure, the particular flavor
that I call Carriego and that allows us to pick out one
face in a crowd. Be that as it may, such a store of inconsequential memories—his tone of voice, the way
he walked, the way he idled, the expression in his
eyes—is that part of my information about him
which least lends itself to the pen. All this is conveyed
only by the word "Carriego," which requires that
both the reader and I possess the very image that I
wish to communicate. There is another paradox. I

have just said that to anyone acquainted with Evaristo Carriego the mere mention of his name is
enough to conjure him up; I now add that any description of Carriego would satisfy them provided it
did not grossly contradict the image they already had
of him. I quote Giusti in the August 1927 issue of
Nosotros: "an emaciated poet with small searching
eyes, always in black, who lived on the edge of
town." The hint of death, present in the words
"always in black" and in the opening adjective, was
also there in his lively face, through which the bone
structure of the skull showed clearly. Life, desperate
life, was in his eyes. Marcelo del Mazo, too, appro-
priately recalled them in his funeral oration, speaking of "the unique expression in his eyes, which held
so little light and yet were so alive."

Carriego came from Paraná, in the province of
Entre Ríos. His grandfather, Evaristo Carriego the
lawyer, was the author of a stiffly bound volume with
creamy paper that was rightly entitled *Forgotten Pages*
(Santa Fe, 1895) and that the reader, if he is in the
habit of browsing in the turgid purgatory of second-
hand books on Lavalle Street, may at some point
have held in his hands. Held and put down, since the
book's passion concerns minutiae. The book consists
of a collection of pages given to taking sides on burning issues in which everything from Latin tags to
Macaulay or Plutarch according to Garnier is roped
in to prove his point. His courage is in his spirit:
when the Paraná legislature decided to erect a statue
of Urquiza during Urquiza's lifetime, the only member to protest, in a beautiful if useless speech, was
Dr. Carriego. The elder Carriego is worthy of mention here not only for his possible polemical legacy
but also for the literary tradition that his grandson

52

would later follow in sketching those first rather weak pages that are the basis of the strong ones.

Carriego was an Entrerriano of several generations' standing. The native Entre Ríos intonation, like the Uruguayan, combines beauty and savagery in the same way that a jaguar does. It is a pugnacious intonation whose symbol is the lance wielded by gaucho militiamen during the civil wars. It is soft: a sultry, yet deadly, and even unashamed softness typifies the most bellicose pages of Leguizamón, of Elías Regules, and of Silva Valdés. It is serious: the Uruguayan Republic, where the intonation I am talking about is more in evidence, has not produced a single humorous page or a single amusing one since the fourteen hundred epigrams written in a Spanish-colonial style by Acuña de Figueroa. When pressed into the service of versifying, the intonation swings between watercolor and felony, lending itself not to the resignation of a Martín Fierro but to the excitement of rum or politics, yet soft-voiced. The sense of trees and Indians lurking in the background, which is inherent in this, is too savage for us Argentines to understand. This seriousness seems to stem from a life harder than our own. Segundo Sombra, a Buenos Aires man, knew the wide-open spaces of the plains, the herding of cattle, and an occasional knife fight; had he been an Uruguayan, he would also have known the cavalry charges of the civil wars, the cruel herding of men, and smuggling. Through tradition, Carriego knew of the old way of life, and he blended it with the sullen ways of the early dwellers of the outer slums.

To the obvious reasons for his Argentineness—a provincial ancestry and the fact that he lived on the edge of Buenos Aires—we should add another paradoxical reason: his trace of Italian blood, expressed in his mother's family name, Giorello. I say this without wishing to offend: the Argentineness of the full-blooded native is inescapable, while that of the person of mixed origin is a decision, a conscious choice. The worship of all things English found in Rudyard Kipling, the "inspired Eurasian journalist"—is this not a further proof (if physiognomy were not enough) of his dusky blood?

Carriego used to boast, "Hating the Italians isn't quite enough for me; I slander them," but the gay abandon of the remark gives the lie to it. The true Argentine, secure in his austerity and in the fact of being in his own home, considers the newcomer Italian a junior. His very happiness is his blessing, his saving grace. It has often been remarked that the Italian can do anything in this country except be taken really seriously by those whom he has displaced. This tolerance, rooted as it is in concealed irony, is the sly revenge of this country's native sons.

The Spaniards were another favorite butt of Carriego's antipathy. The way the Spaniard was generally looked on—as the fanatic who has replaced the Inquisition by the Dictionary of Gallicisms, the servant in a forest of feather dusters*— was also Carriego's view. I need hardly say that this wariness, or prejudice, did not prevent his having several Spanish friends, such as the lawyer Severiano Lorente, who seemed to have brought with him the indolent, generous Spanish attitude toward time (the ample time of the Arabs, who engendered *The Thousand and One Nights*) and who would linger until dawn in the Royal Keller, savoring his half bottle of wine.

Carriego felt an obligation to his run-down neighborhood, an obligation which the knavish fash-

54

ion of that day expressed in terms of bad temper but which Carriego was to regard as a strength. To be poor implies a closer contact with reality, a direct confrontation with the hard knocks of life, a knowledge that the rich seem to lack, as if everything came to them filtered. So indebted did Evaristo Carriego believe himself to be to his environment that on two separate occasions in his work he excuses himself for writing verses to a woman, as if to dwell upon the bitter lot of the poor of his neighborhood were the only legitimate use for his life.

The events of his life, while infinite and incalculable, are outwardly easy to record, and in his book of 1921 Gabriel has helpfully listed them. Here we learn that Evaristo Carriego was born on May 7, 1883, that he completed three years of high school, that he worked on the editorial staff of *La Protesta*, that he died on October 13, 1912, and other detailed and unvisual information with which the author's disjointed work—which should be to make such information visual—liberally burdens the reader. I believe that a chronological account is inappropriate to Carriego, a man whose life was made up of walks and conversations. To reduce him to a list, to trace the order of his days, seems to me impossible; far better seek his eternity, his patterns. Only a timeless description, lingering with love, can bring him back to us.

In a literary context, neither his praise nor his condemnation left any room for doubt. He could be extremely vicious, profaning the most respected names with that obvious perversity that is usually but a bow to the establishment itself, a loyal belief that the present company is faultless and could not be improved upon by the addition of anyone else.

55

The aesthetic capability of words was revealed to him, as to most Argentines, through the sorrows and joys of Almafuerte. This enthusiasm was later borne out by his friendship with Almafuerte. *Don Quixote* was Carriego's preferred reading. As to *Martín Fierro*, he probably did as everyone else in those days—gave it a few avid, secret readings in his boyhood that led to an uncritical love of it. He was also fond of the maligned stories of outlaws and desperadoes produced by Eduardo Gutiérrez, from the semifictional tale of Juan Moreira to the unalloyed real-life account of Hormiga Negra, who hailed from San Nicolás (where the saying is, *"¡del Arroyo y no me arrollo!"*—"from the Drink and I don't shrink!"). France, then the source of all that was fashionable, had made Carriego its spokeman for Georges d'Esparbès, for one or two of Victor Hugo's novels, and for those of Dumas. In addition, in his conversation Carriego admitted a taste for tales of blood and thunder. He was fond of repeating the stories of the death of the gaucho chief Ramírez in the cause of love—he had been speared from his horse and beheaded for defending his woman—and the death of Juan Moreira, who went from the ardent games of the brothel to the bullets and bayonets of the police. Nor did Carriego neglect the events of his own time—the stabbings at local dances or on street corners, tales of knife fights that imbue the teller with their own heroism. "His conversation," Giusti was later to write, "evoked the patios of his neighborhood, its wailing street organs, its dances, its wakes, its toughs, its houses of ill fame, and its flesh destined for prison or hospital. We who were from the center of the city listened to him utterly enchanted, as if he were telling us tales of a far-off country." Carriego knew himself to be frail and mortal, but the endless pink-walled streets of Palermo kept him going.

He wrote little, which means that his drafts were oral. During his nightly walks through the streets, on streetcar platforms, while returning home late, he was always composing verses. The next day—usually after lunch, the hour of the day shot through with languor but free from care—he set them to paper. He never exhausted the night, nor did he ever indulge in the depressing ceremony of getting up early to write. Before submitting what he had written, he would try out its immediate effect by reading it aloud or reciting it to friends. One of these whose name invariably comes up is Carlos de Soussens.

"The night Soussens discovered me," was one of the dates regularly cited in Carriego's conversation. He both liked and disliked Soussens for the same reasons. Carriego liked the fact that Soussens was French, a man associated with the prestige of Dumas *père*, Verlaine, and Napoleon; what troubled Carriego was that Soussens was not far from being an Italian, an immigrant, a man whose dead did not lie in America. Besides, the oscillating Soussens was more of a tentative Frenchman: he was, in his own evasive phrase—which Carriego quoted in a verse— "a gentleman from Fribourg," a Frenchman who never quite managed to be French and never left off being Swiss. In theory, Carriego liked Soussens' complete Bohemian freedom but was troubled—to the point of holding his friend up as a bad example— by Soussens' complicated laziness, his excessive drinking, his habit of putting things off and of lying. These reservations indicate that the Evaristo Carriego of honest Argentine tradition was the real one and not Carriego the night owl, who frequented the Café Los Inmortales.

But Carriego's closest friend was Marcelo del Mazo, who felt for him that almost bewildered admiration that the man of instinct often inspires in the man of letters. Del Mazo, an unjustly forgotten author, practiced in his writing the same controlled politeness as in his daily dealings, and he treated his subjects with great delicacy and compassion. In 1910 del Mazo published *Los vencidos* (second series), a largely unknown book which contains pages that border on the outstanding, such as the diatribe against the elderly—less savage but better observed than Swift's in his *Travels into Several Remote Nations, III,* 10—and another called *"La última."* Other writers who were friends of Carriego were Jorge Borges, Gustavo Caraballo, Félix Lima, Juan Más y Pi, Álvaro Melián Lafinur, Evar Méndez, Antonio Monteavaro, Florencio Sánchez, Emilio Suárez Malimano, and Soiza Reilly.

Let me go on to his neighborhood friendships, of which he had many. The most useful of them was the one with the local political boss Nicolás Paredes, who was then the chief of Palermo. Carriego had sought out this friendship as a boy of fourteen. Wanting to offer his loyalty to someone, he asked for the name of the ward boss, he was given it, he looked the man up, making his way through the burly bodyguards with their high-crowned hats, and told Paredes he was Evaristo Carriego, from Honduras Street. All this happened at the marketplace in Güemes Square; the boy stayed right there until daybreak, rubbing shoulders with toughs and—as gin builds up confidence—men who had killed, calling them by their first names. Elections at the time were settled by brute force, and, to apply this force, the north and south sides of Buenos Aires produced voters in direct proportion to their native-born population and their poverty. This electoral system operated in the province as well. Political bosses of each ward went out where the party needed them, taking their henchmen with them. Eye and steel—crumpled bank notes and penetrating revolvers—cast their independent vote. Implementation of the Sáenz Peña Act,* in 1912, broke up these private armies. But the sleepless night I am talking about is still 1897, and it is Paredes who lays down the law.

Paredes is the true Argentine in all his glory, in total possession of his own reality: the chest swollen with manliness; the masterful presence; the arrogant black mane of hair; the bushy moustache; the normally deep voice which, when he is provoked, he purposely softens into a drawl; the deliberate stride; the use he makes of an anecdote that might flatter him, of strong language, of skillful card playing, of the knife and the guitar; the boundless self-assurance. He is a man who rode horseback as well, having grown up in an earlier Palermo than this one of carriages, in the Palermo of open space and farms. He is a man of Homeric barbecues and interminable sessions of dialogue improvised in song. Thirty years after that fateful night, Paredes was to address to me some stanzas from which I shall never forget this bolt from the blue, this declaration of friendship:

A usté, compañero Borges,
Lo saludo enteramente.

[You, friend Borges, I greet wholeheartedly.]

He is peerless with the knife, but any tough out to offend him has been kept in line by the imperious whip or his open hand and not knife to knife as an equal. Friends, like the dead and like cities, help make up a man, and there is a line in Carriego's "El alma del suburbio" (Soul of the Slums), from the poem "El guapo" (The Tough)—"since he has already once made him sh . . . ake in his boots"—in which Paredes' voice seems to rumble with that weary, almost bored, thunder of true Argentine abuse.

Through Nicolás Paredes, Evaristo Carriego got to know the knife fighters of the district, the cream of the spare-us-from-them ilk. For a time he kept up an unequal friendship with them, a ritual Argentine friendship, with barroom effusiveness and gaucho oaths of loyalty and "you know me, old buddy" and other such inanities. The ashes of these acquaintances are the few stanzas in *lunfardo* that Carriego failed to sign, two sets of which I have tracked down. One thanks Félix Lima for sending him his collection of chronicles, *Con los nueve*; the other, whose title may be a mimicry of the Dies Irae, is called "Día de bronca." It was published in the police gazette *L.C.* under the pen name "The Burglar," and I have included it in the supplement to this chapter.

Nothing is known of any love affair he may have had. His brothers recall a woman in mourning who used to wait for him on the sidewalk and who sent any passing boy to fetch him. Although his brothers ragged him, they never got her name out of him.

I arrive at the matter of his illness, which I regard as of paramount importance. It is the general belief that tuberculosis killed him. This opinion was contradicted by his family, who were perhaps influenced by two superstitions—one, that the disease is shameful; the other, that it is hereditary. Apart from his relatives, everyone contends that he died of consumption. Three considerations bear out the consensus of his friends: the inspired variety and liveliness of Carriego's conversation, a gift possibly owed to a feverish condition; the constant, almost obsessive allusion in his work to red sputum; his compelling need for applause. He knew that he was pledged to death and that no other immortality was open to him than that of his writing; hence his impatience for glory. In the café, he forced his verses on his friends, he led the conversation toward subjects that touched on those he had written poems about, he damned with faint praise or with total condemnation those colleagues of his who were dangerously gifted; as if absentmindedly, he would speak of "my talent." In addition, he had made up or borrowed a sophism which predicted that the entire corpus of contemporary poetry was going to perish because of its rhetoric, except his own, which would survive as a document—as if a fondness for rhetoric were not one of the very hallmarks of the century. "He was perfectly right to make it his business to draw attention to his work," writes del Mazo. "Carriego realized that recognition is a very slow process and is attained in life only by a handful of old men, and, knowing that he was not going to produce a mass of books, he opened the minds of those around him to the beauty and gravity of his poetry." This was not a sign of vanity; it was the mechanics of glory, it was a task of the same order as that of correcting proof sheets. The unrelenting premonition of death spurred him on. Carriego deeply desired others to give him their time in the future, their affection after he was gone. In the course of this abstract dialogue with souls he came to ignore love and new friendships, limiting himself to being his own publicist and apostle.

Let me introduce a story here. An Italian woman fleeing from her husband's blows, her face bloodied, burst into the patio of the Carriego family one evening. Carriego rushed out furiously into the street and delivered the few necessary strong remarks. The husband, a neighboring bartender, took them without answering, but he held a grudge. Knowing that fame, however embarrassing, is a thing of prime importance, Carriego published a highly censorious piece in *Última Hora* about the Italian's brutality. Its results were immediate: the man, his brutish behavior publicly acknowledged, gave up the grudge amid everyone's flattering smirks; the victimized woman went about smiling for days; and Honduras Street felt it had acquired more substance when it saw itself in print. A person thus able to detect the hidden appetite for fame in others surely suffered from it himself.

The desire to live on in the memory of others dominated him. When some epoch-making pen decided that Almafuerte, Lugones, and Enrique Banchs already made up the triumvirate—or should it be the tricorn or the trimester?—of Argentine poetry, Carriego suggested in café circles the deposition of Lugones in order that the inclusion of himself should not disturb this threefold arrangement.

Variety became rarer; all his days became a single day. Until his death he lived at Number 84 Honduras Street (today Number 3784). He never missed a Sunday at our house on his return from the racetrack. Thinking back on the patterns of his daily life—the unpleasant business of waking up in the morning, the fun of romping about with the younger children, the large glass of Uruguayan cherry brandy or of orange liqueur in the nearby bar on the corner of Charcas and Malabia, long sessions downtown in the bar at Venezuela and Perú, friendly argument, Italian-style meals at La Cortada, the solemn recitation of poems by Gutiérrez Nájera and Almafuerte, the customary manly visit to some house whose entranceway was as rosy pink as a girl, the plucking of a sprig of jasmine on passing by a wall, the habit and the love of night—I detect, in its very ordinariness, a feeling of intimacy and closeness. Such activities are common to us all, are shared by us all. These patterns in Carriego's life that I have described will, I know, bring him closer to us. They repeat him over and over in us, as if Carriego went on living in our lives, as if for a few seconds each one of us were Carriego. I believe that this is literally the case, and that these fleeting moments of becoming him (not of mirroring him), which annihilate the supposed flow of time, are proof of eternity.

To surmise an author's predilections from his books seems an easy thing to do, especially if we forget that he usually states not his own preferences but something of less moment, something he imagines is expected of him. Those adequate though hazy images of the pampa from on horseback, which are always in the background of Argentine consciousness, must also have been present in Carriego. He would have liked to have lived in these images. Other random images, however (at first by chance at home, later intentionally sought out, and finally clung to out of affection), were the ones that would preserve his memory: the patio, a place for serenity, a rose for one's days; a modest St. John's Night bonfire, wallowing like a dog in the middle of the street; the wood-and-coal merchant's sign, the compact heap of blackness, the stacks of wood; the iron door of a tenement house; the men lounging on street corners. These images acknowledge and allude to him. I hope Carriego understood it this way, happily and philosophically, on one of his last nighttime walks through the streets. I imagine that man is receptive to death and that its proximity often permeates him, now with repugnance and now with clarity, now with miraculous perception and farsightedness.

III.
Heretic Masses

Before we take up Carriego's *Misas herejes* it may be worth stressing that every writer starts out with a naïvely physical idea of what art is. To him a book is not an expression or a chain of expressions but literally a *volume*, a prism with six rectangular faces which is made up of thin sheets of paper and which must have a title page, a half title, an epigraph in italics, a foreword in larger italics, a number of parts whose opening words are in small capitals, a table of contents, an ex libris with a small hourglass and a Latin motto, an errata slip, some blank leaves, a leaded colophon, and a printer's device—items generally known to make up the art of writing. Some stylists (usually those of the inimitable past) offer as well a publisher's foreword, a dubious portrait, a facsimile autograph, a variant text, a weighty critical apparatus, publisher's advertisements, a list of works consulted, and some lacunae, but it should be understood that these are not for everyone. The confusion of Holland paper with style, of Shakespeare with Jacobo Peuser (a Buenos Aires publisher), arises from common indolence and persists—only slightly polished up—among rhetoricians, to whose simple acoustical souls a poem is a display case of stresses, rhyme schemes, elisions, diphthongs, and other linguistic fauna. I mention these trivia characteristic of all first books so as to underline the unusual virtues of the one I am about to discuss.

It would be foolish, however, to deny that *Misas herejes* is an apprentice book. In saying this, I am referring not to any lack of skill but to two particular tendencies—the author's almost voluptuous delight in certain words, usually words to do with radiance and authority, and his simple, ambitious determination to define eternal facts for the nth time. There is no fledgling versifier who does not attempt to define the night, a storm, carnal desire, the moon—things that stand in no need of definition since they already have a name or a representation known to us all. Carriego falls in with these two practices.

Neither can he be cleared of the accusation of imprecision. The discrepancy between the incoherent wordiness of compositions—or, rather, decompositions—such as "Las últimas etapas" (The Last Stages) and the conciseness of later work such as "La canción del barrio" (Song of the Neighborhood), is so obvious that it should be neither overstressed nor overlooked. To associate that particular weakness of Carriego's with Symbolism is deliberately to disregard the aims of Laforgue or Mallarmé. We need not go so far afield: the true father of this imprecision was the renowned Rubén Darío, a poet who in exchange for importing certain goods from the French freely fitted out his verses from the *Petit Larousse,* doing so with such an utter disregard for scruples that the words "pantheism" and "Christianity" were synonymous to him and that wanting to signify "boredom" he wrote "nirvana."[1] The amusing thing is that José Gabriel, the formulator of Symbolist etiology, insists on finding symbols all through *Misas herejes*, and on page 36 of his book he treats his readers to this rather insoluble solution to the sonnet "El clavel" (The Carnation):

> [Carriego] means to say that he tried to kiss a woman, and that she, unyielding, placed her hand between their mouths (and this does not become clear until after some considerable effort); but no, to say it in this way would be pedestrian, would not be poetic, so he calls her lips "carnation" and "red herald of amatory declarations," and the woman's act of refusal the execution of the carnation by "the guillotine of her noble fingers."

So much for his explication. Here is the sonnet itself:

> *Fue al surgir de una duda insinuativa*
> *cuando hirió tu severa aristocracia,*
> *como un símbolo rojo de mi audacia,*
> *un clavel que tu mano no cultiva.*
>
> *Hubo quizá una frase sugestiva*
> *o advirtió una intención tu perspicacia,*
> *pues tu serenidad llena de gracia*
> *fingió una rebelión despreciativa.*

---

1. I preserve these impertinences in order to punish myself for having written them. At the time, I thought Lugones' poetry better than Darío's. I also thought Quevedo's better than Góngora's (*1954 footnote*).

Y así, en tu vanidad, por la impaciente
condena de tu orgullo intransigente,
mi rojo heraldo de amatorios credos

mereció, por su símbolo atrevido,
como un apóstol o como un bandido,
la guillotina de tus nobles dedos.

[It was as a result of a creeping doubt that your stern
nobility was wounded by that red symbol of my
boldness, a carnation which your hand does not cul-
tivate.

Perhaps there was a suggestive word, or your intuition sensed an intention, for your graceful serenity
scornfully feigned rebellion.

And so, in your vanity, by the abrupt condemnation
of your stiff pride, my red herald of amatory
declarations—

by its daring symbolism—warranted, like an apostle
or a thief, the guillotine of your noble fingers.]

The carnation is without a doubt a real one, an
ordinary common flower crumpled by the girl, and
the symbolism (the mere Gongorism) is that of the
Spanish explicator, who turns the carnation into lips.

It cannot be denied that by far the greater part
of *Misas herejes* has seriously inconvenienced the
critics. How in the slums' own poet is such innocu-
ous lust to be explained? I think I can answer this
scandalized question as follows: Evaristo Carriego's
tenets coincide with those of the slum neighborhood
itself, not in the superficial sense of using it for subject
matter, but in the genuine sense that this is the sort

of poetry the outer slums produce. Poor people relish this sorry rhetoric, a fondness they do not usually extend to realistic descriptions of themselves. The paradox is as wondrous as it is unconscious: the fact that a writer is genuinely of the people is argued on the grounds of the only pages of that writer that common people like. That liking is owed to an affinity: the wordiness, the string of abstractions, the mushiness are the marks of the poetry of the slums, which is uninfluenced by any local accent except the gauchesco, and is closer to Joaquín Castellanos and Almafuerte than to tango lyrics. Memories of certain street corners and bars come to my aid here: the slums draw on *arrabalero*, a bogus version of the thieves' argot, which is *lunfardo*, that is spoken downtown on Corrientes Avenue, but the high-flown abstraction is its own and is the material with which the popular ballad singer works. Let me sum up briefly. This erring portion of *Misas herejes* does not mention Palermo, but Palermo could have produced it. This din demonstrates it:

> *Y en el salmo moral, que sinfoniza*
> *un salvaje ciclón sobre la pauta,*
> *venga el robusto canto que presagie,*
> *con la alegre fiereza de una diana*
> *que recorriese como un verso altivo*
> *el soberbio delirio de la gama*
> *el futuro cercano de los triunfos,*
> *futuro precursor de las revanchas;*
> *el instante supremo en que se agita*
> *la visión terrenal de las canallas . . .*

[And in the moral psalm, which a fierce cyclone symphonizes on the stave, let there come the robust song that will foretell, with the sprightly violence of a bugle call that like a haughty verse runs up and down the delirium of the scale, the imminent future of the victories, a future foretelling revenge; the supreme moment in which the earthly vision of the rabble is stirred up . . .]

All of which adds up to a storm made into a psalm that is to contain a song that is to resemble a bugle call that is to resemble a verse, and the prediction of an immediately foretelling future entrusted to the song that is to resemble the bugle call that is to resemble a verse. To prolong this quotation would be tantamount to bearing a grudge. Take my word for it that this rhapsody of a ballad singer drunk on hendecasyllables exceeds two hundred lines and that not one of its many stanzas can bewail a lack of storms, flags, condors, bloodstained bandages, and hammers. May any unpleasant memory of them be erased by the following ten-line stanzas, in which the passion is sufficiently detailed for us to consider them autobiographical and which lend themselves so well to a guitar accompaniment:

> *Que este verso, que has pedido,*
> *vaya hacia ti, como enviado*
> *de algún recuerdo volcado*
> *en una tierra de olvido . . .*
> *para insinuarte al oído*
> *su agonía más secreta,*
> *cuando en tus noches, inquieta*
> *por las memorias, tal vez,*
> *leas, siquiera una vez,*
> *las estrofas del poeta.*

> *¿Yo . . . ? Vivo con la pasión*

de aquel ensueño remoto,
que he guardado como un voto,
ya viejo, del corazón.
Y sé en mi amarga obsesión
que mi cabeza cansada
caerá, recién, libertada
de la prisión de ese ensueño
¡cuando duerma el postrer sueño
sobre la postrer almohada!

[May these lines, which you have asked for, go to you, as if sent by some memory washed up on the shores of oblivion, to whisper in your ear their most secret agony when at night, restless with memories, perhaps you will read, if only once, these stanzas of mine.

Me? I live with the passion of that dream of long ago, which I have kept like a promise, now grown old, of my heart. And I know in my bitter obsession that my weary head will only rest, freed from that imprisoning dream, when I sleep my last sleep on my last pillow!]

I now pass on to the realistic pieces that make up the section of *Misas herejes* called "El alma del suburbio," in which at last we can hear Carriego's true voice, so noticeably absent from the book's weaker parts. I shall take them in order, intentionally omitting two—"De la aldea" (From the Village), a sketch of Andalusian inspiration and decidedly trivial; and "El guapo," which I shall leave for a later and fuller discussion.

The first poem, "El alma del suburbio," tells about an evening on a street corner. Carriego describes a teeming street turned patio, the consolation of simple things, which is the only possession of the poor: the useful magic of playing cards, human contact, the barrel organ with its habanera and its Italian, the drawled insolence of street cries, the endless argument that leads nowhere, the subjects of women and death. Nor did Carriego forget the tango, which was danced lewdly and raucously on the sidewalks as if straight from the whorehouses of Junín Street, and which, like the knife fight, was the exclusive paradise of men:[2]

En la calle, la buena gente derrocha
sus guarangos decires más lisonjeros,
porque al compás de un tango, que es La Morocha,
lucen ágiles cortes dos orilleros.

[People in the street are lavish with vulgar approval, for to the rhythm of the tango "La Morocha" two men from the outer slums are showing off suggestive dance steps.]

Next comes a poem of mysterious renown, "La viejecita" (The Old Woman). Highly praised when it was first published, this piece's slight touch of

---

2. A detailed history of the tango has already been written. Its author is Vicente Rossi; its title is *Cosas de negros* (1926), a work that is destined to become a classic of Argentine literature and that, by virtue of its sheer stylistic brilliance, will be found correct in all its judgments. To Rossi, the tango is Afro-Montevidean, from the docks, and in its roots has African features. To Laurentino Mejías (*La policía por dentro*, II, Barcelona, 1913) it is an Afro–Buenos Aires hybrid, originating in the monotonous *candombes* of the parishes of Concepción and Monserrat and later hooliganized in the dives of Lorea, the Boca del Riachuelo, and Solís. It was also danced in the houses of ill fame of Temple Street, the smuggled-in barrel organ muffled by a mattress borrowed from one of the venal beds, and the weapons of those present hidden in the neighboring sewers against a possible police raid.

realism—nowadays scarcely perceptible—was only marginally stronger than that of other rhapsodies of the period. By the same facility with which they serve up praise, critics run the risk of becoming prophets. The superlatives attached to "La viejecita" would later be merited by "El guapo"; the acclaim that Ascasubi's *Los mellizos de la flor* received in 1862 is a perfect prophecy of *Martín Fierro*.

"Detrás del mostrador" (Behind the Bar) is about the contrast between the demanding, noisy life of drunkards and the beautiful, coarse woman walled off

detrás del mostrador, como una estatua

[behind the counter, like a statue]

who, undaunted, drives their desire to a frenzy:

Y pasa sin dolor, así, inconsciente,
su vida material de carne esclava:

[And in this way, painlessly, unaware, she lives out her life of flesh enslaved:]

the obscure tragedy of a soul that does not know of its own existence.

The following poem "El amasijo" (The Beating), is the exact opposite of "El guapo." In the former, the seamier side of life is exposed with holy wrath: the hoodlum at home, the double misfortune of the woman, beaten and derided, and of the hoodlum persisting disgracefully and stubbornly in that poor vain manliness, tyranny:

73

Dejó de castigarla, por fin cansado
de repetir el diario brutal ultraje
que habrá de contar luego, felicitado,
en la rueda insolente del compadraje. . . .

[He stopped beating her, tired in the end of repeating the daily brutal outrage that he would later brag
of, congratulated, among his gang of swaggering
cronies. . . .]

The engaging subject of the next poem, "En el
barrio" (In the Neighborhood), is the eternal one of
the guitar and the ballads sung to it, uttered this time
not in the usual conventional way but literally to express an actual love. The action, or what lies behind
the images, is unclear, but it is strong. From the in-
nermost earthen patio, or red patio, the compelling
milonga calls out with passionate rage

que escucha insensible la despreciativa
moza, que no quiere salir de la pieza . . .

.   .   .   .

Sobre el rostro adusto tiene el guitarrero
viejas cicatrices de cárdeno brillo
en el pecho un hosco rencor pendenciero
y en los negros ojos la luz del cuchillo.

.   .   .   .

Y no es para el otro su constante enojo.
A ese desgraciado que a golpes maneja
le hace el mismo caso, por bruto y por flojo,
que al pucho que olvida detrás de la oreja.

Pues tiene unas ganas su altivez airada
de concluir con todas las habladurías.

74

¡Tan capaz se siente de hacer una hombrada
de la que hable el barrio tres o cuatro días! . . .

[that the contemptuous girl listens to unmoved, not
wanting to leave her room.

.   .   .   .

On his grim face the guitarist bears old scars with a
livid sheen, in his breast a sullen, contentious ven-
om, and in his black eyes the glint of a knife.

.   .   .   .

And his continued anger is not toward his rival. To
that miserable creature, whom he can handle with
his fists, he pays the same attention, whether rough
or gentle, as to the cigarette end he has forgotten
behind his ear.

In his irate arrogance he wants to be done with all
the idle gossip. He feels quite competent to take a
manly stand that will give the neighborhood something to talk about for three or four days.]

This last stanza, the penultimate of the poem, is
dramatic in tone; it seems to be spoken by the
scarred man himself. The last line, too, is quite
pointed—the few days' hasty attention that the
neighborhood, spoiled back then, gave a death, the
passing glory of having slit someone's throat.

Next comes "Residuo de fábrica" (Factory
Waste), a compassionate account of suffering, in
which perhaps the most important thing is the in-
stinctive conversion of an illness into a defect, a
fault.

Ha tosido de nuevo. El hermanito

que a veces en la pieza se distrae
jugando, sin hablarle, se ha quedado
de pronto serio, como si pensase . . .

Después se ha levantado, y bruscamente
se ha ido, murmurando al alejarse,
con algo de pesar y mucho de asco:
—Que la puerca otra vez escupe sangre . . .

[She has another coughing fit. Her little brother, who occasionally amuses himself in the room playing, without a word to her, suddenly becomes serious, as if he were thinking . . .

Then he gets up and abruptly leaves, mumbling with a little sympathy and a lot of revulsion, "I hope the pig spits up blood again."]

It seems to me that the emotional emphasis in the poem's penultimate stanza is in the cruel detail "without a word to her."

Now comes "La queja" (The Lament), which is a tedious anticipation of countless tedious tango lyrics, a life story of the splendor, the fading, the downfall, and the obscure end of a prostitute. The subject can be traced back to Horace—Lydia, the first of this endless sterile lineage, goes mad with burning solitude just as mares go mad (*"matres equorum"*), and in her long since deserted room *"amat ianua limen,"* the door hugs the threshold—and flows into Contursi, passing through Evaristo Carriego, whose South American harlot's progress, rounded off by tuberculosis, is of little importance in the sequence.

The next poem is "La guitarra" (The Guitar), an aberrant series of silly images unworthy of the author of "En el barrio." The piece seems to scorn or to be unaware of the poetic effects that the instrument can inspire: the music generously given to the street, the happy melody that is sad to us because of the memory of an incident we associate with it, the friendships that a guitar fosters and crowns. I have seen two men make friends, their souls keeping pace as they played a *gato** that reflected the joyous sound of their coming together.

The last of the poems is "Los perros del barrio" (The Neighborhood Dogs), which is a dull echo of Almafuerte, but which is based on real fact, since in their poverty these outlying slums always had dogs in plenty, either because of their usefulness as watchdogs or out of curiosity about their habits, which is a pastime one never tires of, or out of negligence. Carriego unduly allegorizes this lawless beggarly pack, but at the same time he gives us a feeling of its warm gregarious life, its lowly appetites. I want to quote the line

cuando beben agua de luna en los charcos

[when they drink moon water in puddles]

and another,

aullando exorcismos contra la perrera,

[howling exorcisms against the dog pound,]

which tugs on one of my most vivid memories: the absurd affliction of that little inferno heralded by forlorn barking and preceded—shortly before—by a dusty cloud of poor children who, with shouts and

77

stones, scare off another dusty cloud, of dogs, to save them from the dogcatcher.

What remains to be considered is "El guapo," a paean with a famous dedication to another political tough of Alsina's,* *Saint* Juan Moreira. It is a devout offering,[3] whose power also resides in oblique references, as in the line

conquistó, a la larga, renombre de osado

[he won, in the end, a reputation for his daring]

implying that there had been many competitors for this reputation, and in this line of erotic power almost suggestive of magic:

caprichos de hembra que tuvo la daga.

[a knife's womanly capriciousness.]

In "El guapo" even the omissions are important. The tough was neither a holdup man nor brutally cruel, nor was he necessarily a bully; he was just as Carriego defined him, "a cultivator of courage." At best a stoic, at worst he was an expert in making a big noise, a specialist in stepped-up intimidation, a veteran of winning without ever fighting. He was worthier by far than his present-day degenerate Italian counterpart, a "cultivator of villainy," a petty criminal pained by the shame of not being a pimp. Addicted to the intoxication of danger, a foregone winner by his presence alone—these, with no sug-

---

3. Marred only in the last two lines by the arbitrary mention of the musketeer.

gestion of cowardice in the latter, were the tough. (If a community decides that courage is the principal virtue, the pretension to courage will be as prevalent as the pretension to beauty among women or to imagination among writers, but that selfsame appearance of courage becomes an apprenticeship.)

I am talking about the old-time tough, a Buenos Aires character who appeals to me far more than that other more popular myth of Carriego's (Gabriel, page 57), "the back-street seamstress who came to grief" and her physical-emotional problems. His occupation was that of either teamster, horsebreaker, or slaughterhouse worker; his education, any of the city's street corners, particularly, on the Southside, the Alto (those within the bounds of Chile, Garay, Balcarce, and Chacabuco streets) and, on the Northside, Tierra del Fuego (those within the bounds of Las Heras, Arenales, Pueyrredón, and Coronel streets), and other neighborhoods, such as the Once, the Batería, and the old Stockyards.[4] He was not always

---

4. His name? I offer to legend this list, which I owe to the kind helpfulness of don José Olave. It covers the final two decades of the last century. It will always conjure up an adequate, if blurred, picture of knife-fighting half-breeds as lean and hard as cacti in the dusty outer slums.

PARISH OF OUR LADY OF SUCCOR
Avelino Galeano (of the Provincial Guards Regiment). Alejo Albornoz (killed in a fight in Santa Fe Street by the hereinafter named). Pío Castro.
Footpads, hired toughs: Tomás Medrano, Manuel Flores.

PARISH OF EL PILAR, ANTIGUA
Juan Muraña. Romualdo Suárez, alias "El Chileno." Tomás Real. Florentino Rodríguez. Juan Tink (of English origin, who ended up a police inspector in Avellaneda). Raimundo Renovales (slaughterhouse worker).

(continued)

a rebel: political parties hired the fear he generated and his skill with a knife, and at the same time they gave him their protection. The police, in those days, treated him with kid gloves. In any disturbance the tough never let himself be rounded up, but he gave—and kept—his word to turn himself in later on. The protective influence of the political party took the unpleasantness out of this ritual. Feared as he was, the tough never thought of giving up his way of life: a horse decked out in showy silver, a few pesos for the cockfights or cards—these were enough to brighten his Sundays. He did not have to be physically strong; one of the toughs of the First Precinct, Shorty Flores, was a midget as skinny as a snake, a dead loss, but with a knife he was streaked lightning. The tough did not have to be a troublemaker; the renowned Juan Muraña was a reliable fighting machine, a man with no other distinguishing features than the deadly certainty of his arm and an absolute incapacity for fear. The tough did not know when to make a move and with his eyes—slavish soul that he was—asked the permission of his boss of the moment. Once he was involved in a fight, all his lunges

---

Footpads, hired toughs: Juan Ríos. Damasio Suárez, alias "Carnaza."

PARISH OF BELGRANO

Atanasio Peralta (killed fighting several opponents). Juan González. Eulogio Muraña, alias "Cuervito."

Footpads: José Díaz. Junto González.

They never fought in gangs but always with a naked blade and alone.

The British contempt for the knife has become so widespread that I can rightly recall the commonly held idea that for the Argentine the only serious way of fighting, among men, was that carrying the risk of death. A punch was a mere prologue to the use of steel, an act of provocation.

were for the kill. He did not want to "feed the crows." He spoke without fear or favor of the deaths he had notched up—or rather, that fate had accomplished through him, for there are acts of such heavy responsibility (that of begetting a man or killing a man) that to feel remorse or to boast of them is folly. He died in old age with his constellation of deaths by then, no doubt, dim in his memory.

IV.
Song of the Neighborhood

Nineteen hundred and twelve. Out toward the many stock pens of Cerviño Street or toward the canebrakes and potholes of the Maldonado—an area reduced to galvanized-iron sheds, variously named dance halls, where the tango was all the rage at ten cents a dance, partner included—local toughs still tangled with each other, and now and then a man's face got marked up or a dead hoodlum would be found at dawn, contemptuous, with a slashed belly; but for the most part Palermo conducted itself in a God-fearing manner, and it was a place of genteel poverty, like any other mixed community of immigrants and native Argentines. By this time, the astrological jubilation of the centenary of Argentine independence was already as dead as its miles and miles of blue bunting, as its successions of toasts, its gushing rockets, its municipal illuminations against the rust-colored sky of the Plaza de Mayo, and that other foretold illumination, Halley's comet, was an angel of air and fire to which the organ grinders sang the tango "Independencia." Now sports were of more interest than death, and boys neglected fencing with knives in favor of attending football matches, which in their lazy vernacular they rebaptized *foba.* Palermo joined the rush toward foolishness. Sinister Art Nouveau architecture sprouted like a swollen flower even as far out as the marshes. Noises were different too. The bell of the movie house—which by now had its double features of American Westerns and European love stories—mingled with the tired clatter of horse-drawn wagons and with the knife grinder's whistle. With the exception of a few back alleys there were no unpaved streets. The population had doubled. The 1904 census recorded a total of 80,000 souls within the bounds of Las Heras and Palermo de San Benito; in 1914 it would record 180,000. The electric streetcar screeched around bored street corners. In the popular imagination, Cattaneo, the aviator, had displaced the outlaw Moreira. This almost invisible Palermo, fond of maté and of progress, is the one described in the series of poems that Carriego called "La canción del barrio" (Song of the Neighborhood).

Carriego published "El alma del suburbio" in 1908, and on his death in 1912 he left the material for "La canción del barrio." This latter title is better in its focus and truer to life than the former. *Canción* is more definite than *alma,* and *suburbio* is a term of wariness that has in it something of the anxiety of a man about to miss the last train. Nobody says, "I live in such-and-such a suburb"; everyone prefers to name his *barrio,* or neighborhood. This reference to the neighborhood is just as personal, helpful, and unifying in the parish of La Piedad as it is in Saavedra. The distinction is relevant. To define aspects typical of this country by words relating to an

83

environment derives from a tendency of ours to drag along with us traces of barbarism. The countryman is defined by the pampa; the hoodlum, by certain sheds of old corrugated iron. An example of this may be found in a book by the journalist, or Basque artifact, J. M. Salaverría, which is mistaken right from its title—*El poema de la pampa, Martín Fierro y el criollismo español* (Martín Fierro, the Poem of the Pampa and Spanish Criollism). "Spanish criollism" is a trumped-up piece of nonsense intended to dumbfound the reader (in logic, a *contradictio in adjecto*); "poem of the pampa" is another, less deliberate mistake. According to Ascasubi, "pampa" meant to the old-time country people the wilderness where the Indians marauded.[1] One has only to look into *Martín Fierro* to see that it is the poem not of the pampa but of a man banished to the pampa, of a man rejected by the cattle-breeding civilization centered in ranches that were like villages and in the more populated parts of the countryside. To Martín Fierro, who was the epitome of courage, it hurt to have to endure the solitude—in other words, the pampa.

> *Y en esa hora de la tarde*
> *en que tuito se adormece,*
> *que el mundo dentrar parece*
> *a vivir en pura calma,*
> *con las tristezas de su alma*
> *al pajonal enderiece.*

. . . .

---

1. Today "pampa" is exclusively a literary term; used in the country, it would call attention to itself.

Es triste en medio del campo
pasarse noches enteras
contemplando en sus carreras
las estrellas que Dios cría,
sin tener más compañía
que su soledá y las fieras.

[And in that evening hour when everything grows drowsy, when the world appears to begin to live in complete calm, with a melancholy heart he goes straight for shelter in a growth of reeds.

.   .   .   .

It is sad in the middle of the plain to spend night after night contemplating in their course the stars that God has bred and to have no company but your solitude and wild animals.]

And these immortal stanzas, which are the most moving point in the story:

Cruz y Fierro de una estancia
una tropilla se arriaron,
por delante se la echaron
como criollos entendidos,
y pronto, sin ser sentidos,
por la frontera cruzaron.

Y cuando la habían pasao,
una madrugada clara,
le dijo Cruz que mirara
las últimas poblaciones;
y a Fierro dos lagrimones
le rodaron por la cara.

[From a ranch Cruz and Fierro rounded up a herd

of horses and, being practical gauchos, drove it before them. Undetected, they soon crossed over the border.

After this was done, early one morning Cruz told Fierro to look back on the last settlements. Two big tears rolled down Fierro's face.]

Another Salaverría*—whose name I do not wish to recall, since I admire the rest of his books—goes on and on about the "ballad singer of the pampa" who "in the shade of an ombu, in the endless calm of the desert, recites to the accompaniment of his Spanish guitar the monotonous *décimas* of *Martín Fierro*." But the writer himself is so monotonous, decimated, endless, Spanish, calm, deserted, and accompanied that he has not noticed that *Martín Fierro* is not written in *décimas*. The tendency to drag along with us traces of barbarism is fairly widespread. Santos Vega (whose entire legend, or so we gather from Lehmann-Nitsche's four-hundred-page study, is that there is a Santos Vega legend) made up, or borrowed, the stanza that says:

Si este novillo me mata
no me entierren en sagrao;
entiérrenme en campo verde
donde me pise el ganao.

[If this bull kills me, don't let them bury me in holy ground; bury me in the green fields, where the cattle can walk all over me.]

His quite obvious idea ("If I am so clumsy in my work, I'll refuse to be buried in a cemetery") has been praised as the pantheistic declaration of a man who, after he dies, wants to be trodden on by cows.[2]

The outer slums, too, suffer from an irritating misrepresentation. *Arrabalero* and the tango supposedly typify the slums. In the previous chapter I described how *arrabalero* is spoken downtown on Corrientes Avenue, and how the outpourings of a weekly magazine like *El Cantaclaro*—which prints the lyrics of hit tangos—of phonograph records, and

---

2. To make of the cowhand an eternal traveler across the pampa is a piece of romantic nonsense; to assert—as our best writer of polemical prose, Vicente Rossi, does—that the gaucho is a "Charrúa warrior turned nomad" is merely to assert that unattached Charrúa Indians were called gauchos. This outdated use of a word explains very little. Ricardo Güiraldes, for his version of the cowhand as wanderer, had to resort to the occupation of drover. Groussac, in a lecture delivered in 1893, speaks of the gaucho in retreat "toward the far south, in what is left of the pampa," but it is common knowledge that no gauchos are left in the far south because there never were any there and that where they still exist is in the vicinity of settlements inhabited by native Argentines. Rather than in any racial aspect (a gaucho might be white, black, half Indian, mulatto, or half Indian and half mulatto), rather than in any linguistic aspect (the gaucho from Rio Grande speaks a Brazilian variety of Portuguese), and rather than in any geographical aspect (vast areas of the provinces of Buenos Aires, Entre Ríos, Córdoba, and Santa Fe are now Italian), the gaucho's distinguishing feature resides in his expertise in an early form of cattle breeding.

It is also the fate of the urban hoodlum to be maligned. Only a hundred years ago, *compadritos* was the name given the poor of Buenos Aires who could not afford to live in the vicinity of the Plaza Mayor, a fact which led to their also being called *orilleros,* or dwellers of the outskirts. They were literally the people. They had a half-acre plot and a house of their own beyond Tucumán or Chile Street or what was then Velarde Street and is now Libertad-Salta. The connotations attached to them were later supplanted by a single idea. Ascasubi, in the revision of his *Aniceto el Gallo*, Number 12, was to write, *"compadrito:* a young bachelor, fond of dancing, of falling in love, and of song." Our unacknowledged viceroy, the imperceptible Monner Sans, made him out to be a "bully, roisterer, and braggart," asking, "Why is it that *compadre* always has a bad connotation to us?" He immediately made

(continued)

87

of the radio spread their stagy jargon to places like Avellaneda or Coghlan. Picking up this fashion is no easy matter. Each new tango written in the would-be popular idiom is a riddle, not to mention the bewildering variants, corollaries, obscure patches, and reasoned disagreement of commentators. The obscurity is only logical. People have no need to add local color to themselves; the imitator argues otherwise, and in using local color he goes too far. Nor, as to music, is the tango the natural expression of the outlying neighborhoods, since it originated in brothels. What is truly characteristic of the city's outer edges is the milonga. The milonga, usually, is a long-drawn-out salutation, a courteous giving birth to flattering words, backed up by the grave rhythms of the guitar. Sometimes, in an unhurried fashion, it tells of deeds of blood, knife fights of long ago, killings that follow a brave, soft-spoken challenge; at other times it takes up the theme of destiny. Its moods and stories are varied; what never varies is the

light of the query, writing, with enviable spelling, faultless wit, etc., "Find out for yourselves." Segovia defines the *compadre* by insult: "a boastful, dishonest, aggressive, and treacherous person." This is an exaggeration. Others confuse *compadrito* with *guarango*. They are wrong; the hoodlum need not be vulgar any more than a cowhand. The *compadrito* is, always, an urban proletarian with pretensions to a certain refinement; his other attributes are his courage, which he makes a display of, his use or invention of coarse expressions, and his clumsy handling of refined words. In matters of clothing, he dressed in the ordinary style of the day, with the addition or accentuation of certain details. Back in the 1890s he favored a soft black hat with a very tall crown that was worn cocked on one side, a double-breasted jacket, French-style trousers with a stripe down the side and slightly gathered in at the cuff, black buttoned or elastic-sided boots with tall heels; now (1929) he prefers a soft gray hat worn way back on his head, a generous neckerchief, a pink or dark red shirt, an unbuttoned jacket, one finger or other stiff with rings, tight trousers, and black boots with a mirrorlike shine and light-colored uppers.

What the cockney is to London, the *compadrito* is to Argentine cities.

singer's tone, a high-pitched nasal drawl with spurts of annoyance, never forced but somewhere between speaking and singing. The tango is subject to time, to the humiliations and adversities of time; the driving force of the milonga is clearly timelessness. The milonga is one of the great conversational genres of Buenos Aires; truco is the other. I will go into truco in another chapter; let me only say here that among the poor "man brings cheer to man," as Martín Fierro's elder son discovered in prison.[3] An anniversary, All Souls' Day, one's saint's day, a national holiday, a christening, St. John's Night, an illness, New Year's Eve—all offer an occasion for socializing. Death gives the wake, an opportunity for general conversation and a visit to the dead person, with the door open to everyone. So obvious is this sociability of poorer people that, to make fun of the recent vogue of holding so-called receptions, Dr. Evaristo Carriego wrote that they greatly resembled wakes. Slums are places of stinking water and back alleys, but they are also the sky-blue balustrade and jasmine spilling over a wall and a canary in a cage.[4] "Considerate people," housewives often say.

---

3. And long before Martín Fierro's son, the god Odin. One of the wise books of the Elder Edda (Hávamál, 47) attributes to him the aphorism "*ma r es manns gaman*," which translates literally as "man is man's joy."

4. It is in its outskirts that you find Buenos Aires' unintentional beauty spots, which are also its only beauty spots—airy, floating Blanco Encalada Street; unfashionable street corners of Villa Crespo, San Cristóbal Sur, and Barracas; the majestic poverty of the area around the Paternal freight yards and Puente Alsina. These tell a great deal more, I believe, than those places built expressly to beautify: the Costanera, the Bathing Beach, the Rose Garden; and the highly praised statue to Carlos Pellegrini, which, with its wallowing flag and tempestuous, chaotic pedestal, seems to have utilized the debris of a bathroom demolition; and Virasoro's reticent little boxes, which, in order not to make a display of their individual bad taste, he hides in unadorned abstinence.

Carriego's poor like to talk. Their poverty is not the hopeless or congenital one of the European poor (at least, not of the Europe of the Russian naturalistic novel) but rather the poverty that puts its trust in the lottery, in backroom politics, in personal connections, in card games and their mysteries, in the modest possibilities of betting on a number, in recommendations, or—lacking any other specific, lowly reason—in sheer hope. A poverty that takes comfort in hierarchies—the Requena family of Balvanera, the Luna family of San Cristóbal Norte—that are engaging by their very capacity to appeal to mystery and that are so well embodied in a certain highly distinguished hoodlum of José Álvarez's: "I was born in Maipú Street—are you with me?—in the house of the Garcías, and I'm used to rubbing shoulders with people and not with trash. All right, then. If you don't know, I'm telling you. I was christened in La Merced, and my godfather was an Italian who ran the corner saloon and who died in the epidemic. Just don't forget that!"

It seems to me that the main drawback of "La canción del barrio" is its emphasis on what Shaw called "mere misfortune or mortality" (*Man and Superman*, page xxxiii). Its poems deal with adversities, and the only thing that makes them serious is cruel fate, which is no more understood by the writer than by the reader. Evil casts no shadow over them, we are not led to a contemplation of the origin of evil, which the Gnostics confronted head on by postulating a spectral, waning godhead, obliged to improvise this world with faulty material. What is missing is Blake's view when he asks the tiger, "Did he who made the Lamb make thee?" Nor is the subject of these poems the man who transcends evil, the man who in spite of having suffered wrongs—and having inflicted them—maintains the purity of his soul. What is missing is the stoic view of Hernández, of Almafuerte, of Shaw once again, and of Quevedo, who writes in the second book of his *Castilian Muses*:

> *Alma robusta, en penas se examina,*
> *Y trabajos ansiosos y mortales*
> *Cargan, mas no derriban nobles cuellos.*

> [A robust soul is tested by suffering, and anguish and mortal cares weigh upon but do not bend a noble head.]

Nor does Carriego show interest in the sublimity of evil, or the dramatic passion of misfortune, or the way vicissitudes compel and in a sense inspire life. This is how Shakespeare saw it:

> *All strange and terrible events are welcome,*
> *But comforts we despise; our size of sorrow,*
> *Proportion'd to our cause, must be as great*
> *As that which makes it.*

Carriego appeals only to our compassion.

Here a point or two must be made. The general view, expressed both orally and in writing, is that this inspiring of pity is the strength and justification of Carriego's work. I must disagree, even if I am alone in my opinion. A poetry that lives off domestic conflicts and indulges in petty tribulations, inventing or recording squabbles so that the reader should deplore them, seems to me a loss, a suicide. Its subject is any wounded feeling, anything upsetting; its style is gossipy and full of the interjections, exaggeration, false commiseration, and premature suspicions that housewives trade in. One distorted view (which I have the decency not to understand) is that this exhibition of wretchedness indicates a generous nature. What it indicates, in fact, is a lack of taste. Pieces such as "Mamboretá" or "El nene está enfermo" (The Baby Is Sick) or "Hay que cuidarla mucho, hermana, mucho" (We've Got to Look After Her, Sister)—so overused for mindless anthologies and for recitations—belong not to literature but to crime. They are a deliberate sentimental blackmail that can be reduced to this formula: "I present you with this bit of suffering; if you are not moved, you have no soul." I quote the end of "El otoño, muchachos" (The Autumn, Lads):

> ¡Qué tristona
> anda, desde hace días, la vecina!
> ¿La tendrá así algún nuevo desengaño?
> Otoño melancólico y lluvioso,
> ¿qué dejarás, otoño, en casa este año?
> ¿qué hoja te llevarás? Tan silencioso
> llegas que nos das miedo.
> Sí, anochece
> y te sentimos, en la paz casera,
> entrar sin un rumor . . . ¡Cómo envejece
> nuestra tía soltera!

[How gloomy these past few days our neighbor is! Is she suffering some new disappointment? Sad and rainy autumn, what will you leave behind in our house this year? What leaf will you take away? You come so silently that you frighten us. Yes, the dark is falling, and we feel your presence in the peace of our home, entering without a sound! How old our spinster aunt is getting!]

This spinster aunt, engendered and foisted on us in the haste of the last line so that autumn can gorge itself on her, is a fair indication of the charity of these pages. Humanitarianism is always inhuman. A certain Russian film illustrates the iniquity of war by showing the wretched death agony of an old nag cut down by bullets—fired, of course, by those who made the film.

This reservation noted (its laudable purpose is to boost and firm up Carriego's fame, proving that it stands in no need of such plaintive pages), I would like to point out at once the real strengths of his posthumous work. It has moments of tenderness, discoveries and perceptions of tenderness, as precise as this one:

> *Y cuando no estén, ¿durante*
> *cuánto tiempo aún se oirá*
> *su voz querida en las casa*
> *desierta?*
> *¿Cómo serán*
> *en el recuerdo las caras*
> *que ya no veremos más?*

[And when they are gone, how much longer will their dear voice be heard in the empty house? How will their faces, which we will no longer see, look in our memory?]

Or this snatch of conversation with a street, this secret innocent possession:

> *Nos eres familiar como una cosa*
> *que fuese nuestra: solamente nuestra.*

[You are as familiar to us as a thing that was ours and ours alone.]

Or as this stream, uttered in a single breath as if it were one long word:

No. Te digo que no. Sé lo que digo:
nunca más, nunca más tendremos novia,
y pasarán los años pero nunca
más volveremos a querer a otra.
Ya lo ves. Y pensar que nos decías,
afligida quizá de verte sola,
que cuando te murieses
ni te recordaríamos. ¡Qué tonta!
Sí. Pasarán los años, pero siempre
como un recuerdo bueno, a toda hora
estarás con nosotros.
Con nosotros . . . Porque eras cariñosa
como nadie lo fue. Te lo decimos
tarde, ¿no es cierto? Un poco tarde ahora
que no nos puedes escuchar. Muchachas,
como tú ha habido pocas.
No temas nada, te recordaremos,
y te recordaremos a ti sola:
ninguna más, ninguna más. Ya nunca
más volveremos a querer a otra.

[No. I mean no. I know what I'm talking about: never, never again will we fall in love, and years will pass but we shall never love again. You see it already. And to think you said, afraid perhaps to find yourself alone, that when you die we wouldn't even remember you. How silly! Oh yes, years will pass, but you will be with us always. With us. . . . Because you were dearer than anyone else. We are

94

telling you this a bit late, aren't we? A bit late now that you can't hear us. There have been few girls like you. Don't be afraid of anything, we will remember you, and we shall remember only you: no other, no other. We shall never again love another.]

The repetition in this poem is similar to that of one by Enrique Banchs ("Balbuceo," in *El cascabel del halcón*, 1909), which, line by line, is infinitely superior. ("I could never tell you how much I love you: how much I love you is like a multitude of stars," etc.) This seems false, however, while Carriego's is genuine.

Carriego's best poem, "Has vuelto" (You Are Back), is also from "La canción del barrio."

Has vuelto, organillo. En la acera
hay risas. Has vuelto llorón y cansado
como antes.
                    El ciego te espera
las más de las noches sentado
a la puerta. Calla y escucha. Borrosas
memorias de cosas lejanas
evoca en silencio, de cosas
de cuando sus ojos tenían mañanas,
de cuando era joven . . . la novia . . . ¡quién sabe!

[You are back, organ grinder. On the sidewalk there are smiles. You are back, plaintive and weary as ever. The blind man waits for you, seated most nights by his door. In silence, he recalls faded memories of distant things, things when his eyes beheld the morning, when he was young, his girl, who knows what!]

The line that gives life to the above is not the last

but the next to last, and I am inclined to believe that Evaristo Carriego placed it there to underplay the emphasis. One of his earliest poems, "El alma del suburbio," had dealt with the same subject, and it is appropriate to compare the old solution there (a realistic picture built on detailed observation) with the clear, conclusive one in which all his favorite symbols are assembled—the back-street seamstress who came to grief, the neighborhood organ grinder, the tumbledown street corner, the blind man, and the moon:

> *Pianito que cruzas la calle cansado*
> *moliendo el eterno*
> *familiar motivo que el año pasado*
> *gemía a la luna de invierno:*
> *con tu voz gangosa dirás en la esquina*
> *la canción ingenua, la de siempre, acaso*
> *esa preferida de nuestra vecina*
> *la costurerita que dio aquel mal paso.*
> *Y luego de un valse te irás como una*
> *tristeza que cruza la calle desierta,*
> *y habrá quien se quede mirando la luna*
> *desde alguna puerta.*
> *. . . Anoche, después que te fuiste,*
> *cuando todo el barrio volvía al sosiego*
> *—qué triste—*
> *lloraban los ojos del ciego.*

[Little barrel organ, you cross the street wearily, grinding out the eternal familiar tune that last year you moaned to the winter moon: with your whiny voice you will sing on the street corner the simple song, the usual one, perhaps the favorite one of our neighbor, the seamstress who got into trouble. And

after a waltz you will move on like a sadness that
crosses the empty street, and from some doorway or
other someone will stay there gazing at the moon.
. . . Last night, after you had gone and all the
neighborhood was still again—how sad it was—the
eyes of the blind man wept.]

Tenderness is the achievement of long years.
Another virtue of passing years, evident in this second book and neither hinted at nor apparent in Carriego's previous book, is a sense of humor. It is a
quality indicative of a sensitive nature. The mean-
spirited never engage in this wholesome, compassionate enjoyment of the weaknesses of others that is
so essential to friendship. It is a quality that goes
hand in hand with love. Soame Jenyns, an English
writer of the eighteenth century, thought, in all rev-
erence, that the allotment of happiness granted the
blessed and the angels derived from an exquisite sense
of the ridiculous.

I quote the following lines by Carriego as an example of a quiet sense of humor:

¿Y la viuda de la esquina?
La viuda murió anteayer.
¡Bien decía la adivina,
que cuando Dios determina
ya no hay nada más que hacer!

[And the widow next door? She died the day before
yesterday. Ah, how right the fortune-teller was to
say that when God makes up His mind nothing can
be done about it!]

The mechanism of this bit of humor is twofold: first,
putting into the mouth of a clairvoyant a rather

unclairvoyant moralism on the inscrutability of Providence; and second, the neighborhood's fatalistic respect, which acknowledges the incident with wisdom.

But the most consciously humorous poem left us by Carriego is "El casamiento" (The Wedding). It is also the most typical of Buenos Aires. "En el barrio" is an almost blatantly Entre Ríos bravura piece; "Has vuelto" is a single fragile moment, a flower of time, of a single evening. "El casamiento," on the other hand, is as distinctively Buenos Aires as Ascasubi's *cielitos* or the Argentine *Faust* or the humor of Macedonio Fernández or the lively, punchy openings of the tangos of Greco, Arolas, and Saborido. Carriego's poem is a very skillful expression of the features found at any humble festivity. There is plenty of the kind of carping that goes on between neighborhood busybodies.

> *En la acera de enfrente varias chismosas*
> *que se encuentran al tanto de lo que pasa,*
> *aseguran que para ver ciertas cosas*
> *mucho mejor sería quedarse en casa.*
>
> *Alejadas del cara de presidiario*
> *que sugiere torpezas, unas vecinas*
> *pretenden que ese sucio vocabulario*
> *no debieran oírlo las chiquilinas.*
>
> *Aunque—tal acontece—todo es posible,*
> *sacando consequencias poco oportunas,*
> *lamenta una insidiosa la incomprensible*
> *suerte que, por desgracia, tienen algunas.*
>
> *Y no es el primer caso. . . . Si bien le extrãna*
> *que haya salido sonso . . . pues en enero*

del año que trascurre, si no se engaña,
dio que hablar con el hijo del carnicero.

[From the opposite sidewalk several gossiping
women who always know what's going on assure us
that in order to see some things one is better off at
home.

Out of earshot of the one who looks like a convict
and who is suggesting smutty things, some of the
neighbors claim that his dirty words should not be
heard by young girls.

Although—as it happens—everything is possible,
and, drawing unwholesome conclusions, one insidi-
ous woman laments the incomprehensible luck that,
unfortunately, some women have.

And this is not the first time. Though it's surprising
that he turned out to be such a fool, since only in
January of this year, as sure as not, she was the talk
of the town for what went on between her and the
butcher's son.]

And there is the wounded pride before the fact, the
almost desperate respectability.

El tío de la novia, que se ha creído
obligado a fijarse si el baile toma
buen carácter, afirma, medio ofendido,
que no se admiten cortes, ni aun in broma.

—Que, la modestia a un lado, no se la pega
ninguno de esos vivos . . . seguramente.
La casa será pobre, nadie lo niega:
todo lo que se quiera, pero decente.—

[The bride's uncle, who has taken it upon himself to see that the dancing stays proper, states, somewhat shocked, that suggestive steps are not allowed—even in fun.

"For, modesty apart, not that any of these louts would know what I'm talking about, this house may be poor—there's no denying that—poor as anything, but respectable."]

And there are the petty squabbles that are forever cropping up:

La polka de la silla dará motivo
a serios incidentes, nada improbables:
nunca falta un rechazo despreciativo
que acarrea disgustos irremediables.

Ahora, casualmente, se ha levantado
indignada la prima del guitarrero,
por el doble sentido, mal arreglado,
del piropo guarango del compañero.

[As sure as anything, the broomstick polka will give rise to serious incidents. There is always one offensive refusal to set off a tiff that cannot be settled.

Now, for instance, indignant, the guitarist's cousin has flounced off over the double meaning, carelessly phrased, of her partner's vulgar compliment.]

And touching sincerity:

En el comedor, donde se bebe a gusto,
casi lamenta el novio que no se pueda
correr la de costumbre . . . pues, y esto es justo,
la familia le pide que no se exceda.

[In the dining room, where everyone is having a drink, the groom half laments the fact that they cannot do as they normally do, since—and it's only right—the family has asked him not to go too far.]

And there is the pacifying role of the tough, who is a friend of the family:

Como el guapo es amigo de evitar toda
provocación que aleje la concurrencia,
ha ordenado que apenas les sirvan soda
a los que ya borrachos buscan pendencia.

Y, previendo la bronca, después del gesto
único en él, declara que aunque le cueste
ir de nuevo a la cárcel, se halla dispuesto
a darle un par de hachazos al que proteste.

[As the tough is anxious to avoid any altercation that could break up the party, he has given orders that only soda water be served to those, already drunk, who are spoiling for a fight.

Anticipating the fury that will arise from this act— the only thing he has done—he makes it known that even if it means going back to jail, he is ready to have it out with anyone who protests.]

The following poems from this book will also endure: "El velorio" (The Wake), written in the same style as "El casamiento"; "La lluvia en la casa vieja" (Rain in the Old House), a statement of the excitement caused by the elements, when rain fills the air in the same way as a cloud of smoke, and every house feels itself to be a fortress; and some of the personal sonnets in a conversational tone from

the cycle called "Íntimas" (Intimate Things). These
are heavy with fate. They are of a serene nature, but
their resignation, or reconciliation, is that which
follows on sorrow. Here is a line from one of them,
pure and magical:

cuando aún eras prima de la luna.

[when you were still a cousin to the moon.]

And there is also this rather revealing statement,
which needs no further elucidation:

Anoche, terminada ya la cena
y mientras saboreaba el café amargo,
me puse a meditar un rato largo:
el alma como nunca de serena.

Bien lo sé que la copa no está llena
de todo lo mejor y, sin embargo,
por pereza quizás, ni un solo cargo
le hago a la suerte, que no ha sido buena . . .

Pero, como por una virtud rara
no le muestro a la vida mala cara
ni en las horas que son más fastidiosas,

nunca nadie podrá tener derecho
a exigirme una mueca. ¡Tantas cosas
se pueden ocultar bien en el pecho!

[Last night, dinner over and while I savored my cof-
fee, I began to meditate at length, my soul serene as
never before.

I know quite well that one's cup is not full of all
that's best, and yet—perhaps out of laziness—I

bring not a single charge against my luck, which has not been good.

But, as by some strange power I do not put on a bad face even in the most troubled times,

never will anyone have the right to expect me to look downcast. So many things can be hidden in the heart!]

One final digression, which will not be a digression for long. Pleasant though they may be, the descriptions of daybreak, of the pampa, and of nightfall that appear in Estanislao del Campo's *Fausto* are somewhat frustrating and inapt, a fault produced at the very outset of the story by a single reference to stage scenery. In Carriego, the unreality of the outlying slums is more subtle. It derives from the unplanned, haphazard nature of the place, of the two-way pull of the plains, with their fields or ranches, and of streets with storied houses; of the tendency of the people who live there to think of themselves as men either of the country or of the city but never as men of the outer slums. It was out of this ambivalent material that Carriego created his work.

V.
Possible Summary

Evaristo Carriego, a boy from an Entre Ríos background, brought up on the outskirts of the Northside of Buenos Aires, set himself the task of rendering that outlying suburb into poetry. In 1908 he published *Misas herejes*, an unpretentious and accessible book that contains ten results of that deliberate aim to be local and twenty-seven uneven samples of verse writing. Some of these have a fine sense of the tragic (''Los lobos'' [The Wolves]), while others show delicate feeling (''Tu secreto'' [Your Secret], ''En silencio'' [In Silence]), but most of them are rather imperceptible. The poems of local observation are the ones that matter. They reflect the notion of courage and daring that the run-down edge of the city has of itself, and they were rightly enjoyed. Examples of that first type are ''El alma del suburbio,'' ''El guapo,'' and ''En el barrio.'' Carriego established himself with these themes, but his need to move his readers led him into a maudlin socialist aesthetic whose unwitting reductio ad absurdum would much later be taken up by the Boedo group. Examples of the second type—"Hay que cuidarla mucho, hermana, mucho," "Lo que dicen los vecinos" (What the Neighbors Say), and "Mamboretá"—by appealing to women for their fame, have completely appropriated attention from the others. Later, he adopted a narrative style that had the additional element of humor, a quality so essential to a poet of Buenos Aires. Examples of this last style—Carriego's best—are "El casamiento," "El velorio," and "Mientras el barrio duerme" (While the Neighborhood Sleeps). Also, in the course of time, he wrote a handful of personal pieces, such as "Murria" (Spleen), "Tu secreto," and "De sobremesa" (After Dinner).

What will Carriego's future be? There is no critical posterity other than a posterity given to making definitive judgments, but to me the facts seem certain. I believe that some of his poems—perhaps "El casamiento," "Has vuelto," "El alma del suburbio," "En el barrio"—will appeal to many generations of Argentines. I believe that Carriego was the first observer of our poorer neighborhoods and that this, in the history of Argentine poetry, is what matters. The first—in other words, the discoverer, the inventor.

Truly I loved the man, on this side idolatry, as much as any.

VI.
Complementary Pages

To Chapter II

Ten-line stanzas in *lunfardo*, published by Eva-
risto Carriego in the police gazette *L.C.* (Thursday,
September 26, 1912) under the pseudonym "The
Burglar."

Compadre: si no le he escrito
perdone . . . ¡Estoy reventao!
Ando con un entripao,
que de continuar palpito
que he de seguir derechito
camino de Triunvirato;
pues ya tengo para rato
con esta suerte cochina:
Hoy se me espiantó la mina
¡y si viera con qué gato!

Sí, hermano, como le digo:
¡viera qué gato ranero!
mishio, roñoso, fulero
mal lancero y peor amigo.

¡Si se me encoge el ombligo
de pensar el trinquetazo
que me han dao! El bacanazo
no vale ni una escupida
y lo que es de ella, en la vida
me soñé este chivatazo.

Yo los tengo junaos. ¡Viera
lo que uno sabe de viejo!
No hay como correr parejo
para estar bien en carrera.
Lo engrupen con la manquera
con que tal vez ni serán
del pelotón, y se van
en fija, de cualquier modo.
Cuando uno se abre en el codo
ya no hay caso: ¡se la dan!

¡Pero tan luego a mi edá
que me suceda esta cosa!
Si es p'abrirse la piojosa
de la bronca que me da.
Porque es triste, a la verdá
—el decirlo es necesario—
que con el lindo prontuario
que con tanto sacrificio
he lograo en el servicio,
me hayan agarrao de otario.

Bueno: ¿que ésta es quejumbrona
y escrita como sin gana?
Échele la culpa al rana
que me espiantó la cartona.
¡Tigrero de la madona,
veremos cómo se hamaca,
si es que el cuerpo no me saca

cuando me toque la mía.
Hasta luego.
—Todavía
tengo que afilar la faca!

[Brother, I'm sorry for not having written. I'm burned up. There is an ache in my guts that, if it goes on, I guess will send me straight down the road to the grave. I've been having a run of bad luck for quite a while. Today my woman walked out on me, and you should see the creep she's with now.

Yes, friend, as I say, you should see this creep— something out of the gutter, a no-good, a dud as a lover, and a worse friend. My belly button shrivels every time I think of the blow they gave me. A dandy like him I wouldn't spit on, and as for her I never dreamed she would cheat on me like this.

I know them inside out. The things you learn with age! Nothing like running steady to stay in the race. They fool you with the pretense that they won't make the finish line, but still they run to win. When they elbow you off the course, it's all over—you've had it!

That this should happen to me—at my age! The rage this puts me in is enough to split my head. Because the sad fact is—and I may as well admit it— that after all my hard work building up a lovely police record I've been had for a stupid fool.

All right, do you think I'm whining here and writing this as if I don't care? Lay the blame on the creep who made off with the silly girl. Damn the trouble-maker, we'll see how he swaggers—if he doesn't steer clear of me, that is—when my turn comes. So long. I'm off to sharpen my knife!]

TRUCO

To Chapter IV

Forty cards are going to stand in for life. In a player's hands, a new pack makes a crisp sound, while an old one sticks clumsily: worthless bits of pasteboard that will come alive, the ace of *espadas* that will be as all-powerful as don Juan Manuel de Rosas, face cards with little round-bellied horses on which Velázquez modeled his. The dealer shuffles these little pictures. The whole thing is easy to describe and even to do, but the magic and the cut-and-thrust of the game—of the playing itself—come out in the action. There are forty cards, and one times two times three times four and on up to times forty are the permutations that can be dealt. It is a figure precisely exact in its enormity, and it has an immediate predecessor and a unique successor, but it is never expressed. It is a remote, dizzying number that seems to dissolve the players into its hugeness. In this way, from the very outset, the game's central mystery is adorned with another mystery: the fact that numbers exist. On the table—bare so that the cards can easily slide—a little pile of chickpeas waits to keep the score, they, too, part of the game's arithmetic. The game begins; the players, turned suddenly into Argentines of old, cast off their everyday selves. A different self, an almost ancestral and vernacular self, takes over the game. In one fell swoop the language changes. Tyrannical prohibitions, clever possibilities and impossibilities, are present in every word. To say *"flor,"* unless you have three cards of the same suit, is a criminal and punishable act, but if somebody else has already said *"envido,"* your *"flor"* is allowable. Once you have made your call you must stick to it; it is a commitment that evolves, phrase by phrase, in euphemisms. *"Quiebro"* means *"quiero," "envite"* means *"envido,"* an *"olorosa"* or a *"jardinera"* mean *"flor."* When a player has a bad hand he may boom out in the voice of a political boss any of these calls: "The game's on, every word counts": *"falta envido"* and *"truco"* or, if someone says *"flor," "¡contraflor al resto!"* The enthusiasm of the dialogue frequently becomes poetry. Truco has formulas to console the loser and verses of jubilation for the winner.

Truco is as evocative as an anniversary. Milongas performed around a campfire or in a saloon, the jollification at wakes, the threatening boasts of the followers of Roca or Tejedor, escapades in the brothels of Junín Street or in their progenitor on Temple Street are the human sources of the game. Truco is a good singer, especially when winning or pretending to be winning; it sings down at the far end of a street in the small hours from lighted barrooms.

In truco, lying is the custom. Its deception is not that of poker—mere impassiveness or unresponsiveness to fluctuation while raising stakes every so many cards. The apparatus of truco is a lying voice, a face that is judged by its expression and that is on the defensive, and tricky and inconsequential phrases. Deceit is raised to an exponential power. A grumbling player who has thrown his cards down on the table could be hiding a good hand (simple ploy), or perhaps he is lying by telling the truth so that we disbelieve it (ploy squared). Leisurely in its pace and full of rambling conversation, the coolness of this Argentine game is part of its cunning. It is a superimposition of masks, and its spirit is that of the street peddlers Moishe and Daniel who met in the heart of the vast Russian steppe.

"Where are you going, Daniel?" said the one.

"To Sebastopol," said the other.

At that, Moishe stared at him and said firmly, "You are lying, Daniel. You say you're going to Sebastopol to make me think you're going to Nizhni Novgorod, when all along you really are going to Sebastopol. You're a liar, Daniel!"

And now a word about the players. They seem to be lost in the clamor of Argentine conversation, trying to scare life off with raised voices. Forty cards—amulets of colored pasteboard, cheap mythology, charms—are enough for the player to conjure away daily life. They try to forget the busy world. The pressing social reality in which we all find ourselves touches on the card game but goes no further; the bounds of its table is another country. Its inhabitants are the *"envido"* and the *"quiero,"* the *"flor"* across the table and the unexpectedness of its gift, the avid series of hands of each game, the seven of *oros* tinkling out hope, and the rest of the passionate lower cards of the pack. Truco players live this little world of hallucination. They keep it going with laconic native sayings, tending it like a fire. It is a narrow world, I am well aware—a phantom of local politics and cunning; a world, after all, invented by stockyard sorcerers and neighborhood necromancers—but not for that any less a substitute for the real world, which is less inventive and diabolical in its ambitions.

To write about a subject as local as that of truco and neither to stray from it nor to delve more deeply into it—the two may amount to the same thing, such is their similarity—strikes me as a serious act of frivolity. At this point I would like to get in a reflection on the limitations of truco. The various stages of its aggressive discourse, its sudden turning points, its flashes of intuition, and its intrigue cannot help but repeat themselves. They must, in the course of time, repeat themselves. For a regular player, what is truco but a habit? Just look at the repetitiveness of the game, at its fondness for set formulas. Every player, in truth, does no more than fall back into old games. His game is a repetition of past games—in other words, of moments of past lives. Generations of Argentines no longer here are, as it were, buried alive in the game. They—and this is no metaphor—are the game. Following this thought through, it transpires that time is an illusion. And so, from truco's labyrinths of colored pasteboard, we approach metaphysics, which is the sole justification and object of any study.

VII.
Inscriptions on Wagons

Imagine a horse-drawn wagon. Imagine a big wagon whose rear wheels, suggestive of reserve power, are taller than its front wheels and whose native-born teamster is as hefty as the wood-and-iron creation on which he rides, his lips pursed in absentminded whistling or, with paradoxically gentle commands, calling out to his team—a shaft pair and a trace horse out front (a jutting prow for those who need the comparison). Loaded or unloaded is all one, except that the pace of the wagon, returning empty, seems less tied to work and the driver's seat more throne-like, as if the wagon still had about it something of the military character of chariots in the marauding empire of Attila. The street the wagon moves through may be Montes de Oca or Chile or Patricios or Rivera or Valentín Gómez, but Las Heras is best because of the variety of its traffic. There the plodding wagon is continually overtaken, but this very lagging becomes its triumph, as if the speed of other vehicles were the anxious scurrying of the slave, whereas the wagon's slowness is a complete possession of time, if not eternity. (Time is the native Argentine's infinite, and only, capital. We can raise slowness to the level of immobility, the possession of space.) The wagon wends its way, a motto inscribed on its side. The authenticity of the city's run-down outskirts demands this, and although these gratuitous bits of expressiveness superimposed on the outward manifestations of physical force—dimension, capacity, actuality—confirm the charge of garrulousness leveled at us by European lecturers, I cannot brush it aside, since it is the gist of this essay. The collection of this stable yard epigraphy, which I have been engaged in for some time, stems from long rambles and idleness that are more poetic than the actual inscriptions, which in these Italianized days are becoming few and far between. I do not mean to dump my whole hoard of penny pieces out on the table but to show just a few. My theme, obviously, is language. We know that those who codified this discipline incorporated into it all the uses of words, even the lowliest and most ridiculous riddle, pun, acrostic, anagram, labyrinth, cubic labyrinth, or emblematic design. If this last, a symbolic figure and not a word, is acceptable, I maintain that the inclusion of legends from wagons cannot be faulted. They are a New World variant of the heraldic motto, the genre born of coats of arms. Besides, the inscriptions on wagons should take their place among other works of literature so that the reader will not be disappointed or expect to find wonders in my roundup. How can I lay claim to wonders here when they cannot be found even in the carefully planned anthologies of Menéndez y Pelayo or Palgrave?

A mistake easily made is that of taking as a genuine motto the name of the firm the wagon belongs to. "Pride of the Bollini Estate," an uninspired name in perfect bad taste, may be an example of this. "Mother of the Northside," a wagon from out in Saavedra, certainly is. A charming name this latter, and it has two possible interpretations. The first, which is unlikely, sees no metaphor and imagines the wagon on its creative way, giving birth to a Northside that burgeons with houses, saloons, and hardware stores. The second, which the reader will have guessed, is that of nurturing. But names like this belong to another and less homely literary genre—the one beloved of business establishments. This genre abounds in masterpieces of compression such as "The Colossus of Rhodes," a tailor shop out in Villa Urquiza, or "The Dormitological," a bedstead factory in Belgrano. This category, however, is outside my sphere.

The genuine wagon inscription is not all that different. By tradition, it makes some simple statement—"The Flower of the Plaza Vértiz," "The Victor"—rather as if it were tired of showing off. Others like this are "The Fish Hook," "The Suitcase," "The Big Stick." The last is beginning to grow on me, but it pales when I remember another motto, also from Saavedra, that tells of extensive journeys like sea voyages, of practical experience among the byways of the pampa and soaring dust storms—"The Schooner."

A distinct species of the genre is the inscription on the smaller wagons of door-to-door peddlers. The haggling and the daily chatter of women have diverted them from a preoccupation with feats of courage, and their gaudy signs tend toward obsequious boasting or flirtation. "Easy Going," "Long Live the One Who Looks After Me," "The Southside Basque," "The Busy Bee," "Tomorrow's Little Milkman," "The Good Looker," "See You in the Morning," "The Talcahuano Champ," and "The Sun Shines for Everyone" are more or less good-humored examples. "What Your Eyes Have Done to Me" and "Where There's Ash There Once Was Fire" show a more individualized passion. "He Who Envies Me Will Die of Despair" is bound to be of Spanish introduction. "Not in Any Hurry" is pure Argentine. The peevishness or the brusqueness of a short phrase is often mitigated not only by a light touch in the wording but by the addition of phrases. I have seen a greengrocer's wagon which, as well as having the presumptuous name "The Neighborhood Favorite," proclaimed in a smug couplet:

Yo lo digo y lo sostengo
Que a nadie envidia le tengo.

[I say this loud and say it bold—I envy no one in the world.]

and annotated the picture of a couple locked together in a suggestive tango with the unambiguous caption "Straight to the Point." Such pithy verbosity, such sententious frenzy, reminds me of the style of the famous Danish statesman Polonius or of that real-life Polonius, the seventeenth-century Spanish writer Baltasar Gracián.

Let me go back to typical inscriptions. "The New Moon of Morón" is the motto on a high-sided wagon that has iron railings like a ship's; I happened to observe it one damp night in the middle of the Buenos Aires Wholesale Market, with its twelve hooves and four wheels lording it over a lavish fermentation of odors. "Lonesomeness" is the name of a wagon that I once saw in the south of the province of Buenos Aires and that speaks of remote stretches. The idea, again, is that of "The Schooner" but more obvious. "What's It to the Old Woman That Her Daughter Loves Me" is impossible to leave out, less for its nonexistent wit than for its pure barnyard touch. The same may be said of "Your Kisses Were for Me," a line from a waltz, which, by being inscribed on a wagon, takes on a note of insolence. "What Are You Staring At, Mr. Green Eyes?" has something of the womanizer and the conceited about it. "I'm Proud," lent dignity by the sun and the driver's high seat, is far better than even the most effusive recrimination from a Boedo street corner. "Here Comes Spider" is a splendid announcement. *"Pa la rubia, cuándo"* (Blondes— When [Never]) is even more splendid, not only for its colloquial clipped ending in the first word and its unstated preference for brunettes but also for its ironic use of the adverb *cuándo* (when), which here stands for *nunca* (never). (I first came across this rejected "when" in a smutty milonga,* which I regret not being able to print under my breath or to tone down decently in Latin. Instead, let me give an example of a similar instance, from Mexico, recorded in Rubén Campos' book *El folklore y la música mexicana:* "They will take from me, they say/the paths I roam along;/the paths may be taken away/ but my cherished haunts, *cuándo." "Cuándo, mi vida"* [My Life—Never], was also the usual verbal sally of those who played at fencing when they parried the burned point of a stick or an opponent's knife.) "The Branch Is in Blossom" is a message of unclouded tranquillity and magic. "Not Much," "You

Should Have Told Me," and "Who Can Have Told" cannot be improved upon. They suggest drama, they are the stuff of daily life, they reflect fluctuations of emotion, and like life they are always there. Written down, they are gestures captured forever, a ceaseless affirmation. Their allusiveness is that of the slum dweller who cannot tell a story plainly or logically but delights in meaningful gaps, in generalizations, and in sidesteps that are as sinuous as a fancy tango figure. But the crowning glory, the dusky flower of this survey, is the mystifying inscription "The Doomed Man Does Not Weep," which kept Xul-Solar and me disgracefully perplexed, although we were accustomed to penetrating the delicate secrets of Robert Browning, the airy intricacies of Mallarmé, and the merely heavy-handed ones of Góngora. "The Doomed Man Does Not Weep." I offer the reader this dark carnation.

There is no basic literary atheism. I once believed I disbelieved in literature, and now I have let myself be led astray by the temptation to collect these fragments of literature. I am justified for two reasons. One is the democratic superstition which takes it for granted that there is merit in any anonymous work, as if all of us together knew what no one of us knows, as if the intellect were self-conscious and performed better unobserved. The other is the facility of judging something short. We are loath to admit that our opinion of a line may not be final. Our faith is placed in lines rather than in chapters. Inevitable at this point is mention of Erasmus, that skeptic and seeker after axioms.

In due course these pages will begin to seem learned. I can provide no other reference to books than a chance paragraph of a predecessor of mine in this regard. The lines belong to those lifeless drafts of classical verse now known as free. This is how I remember them:

Los carros de costado sentencioso
franqueaban tu mañana
y eran en las esquinas tiernos los almacenes
como esperando un ángel.

[Wagons with inscriptions on their sides confirmed the arrival of morning, and on the corners the saloons looked tender, as if awaiting an angel's appearance.]

I prefer those flowers of the stable yard, the inscriptions on wagons.

VIII.
Stories of Horsemen

They are many and they may be countless. My first story is quite modest; those that follow will lend it greater depth.

A rancher from Uruguay had bought a country establishment (I am sure this is the word he used) in the province of Buenos Aires. From Paso de los Toros, in the middle of Uruguay, he brought a horsebreaker, a man who had his complete trust but was extremely shy. The rancher put the man up in an inn near the Once markets. Three days later, on going to see him, the rancher found his horseman brewing maté in his room on the upper floor. When asked what he thought of Buenos Aires, the man admitted that he had not once stuck his head out in the street.

The second story is not much different. In 1903 Aparicio Saravia staged an uprising in the Uruguayan provinces; at a certain point of the campaign, it was feared that his men might break into Montevideo. My father, who happened to be there at the time, went to ask advice of a relative of his, the historian Luis Melián Lafinur, only to be told that there was no danger "because the gaucho stands in fear of cities." In fact, Saravia's troops did change their route, and somewhat to his amazement my father found out that the study of history could be useful as well as pleasurable.[1]

My third story also belongs to the oral tradition of my family. Toward the end of 1870 forces of the Entre Ríos caudillo López Jordán, commanded by a gaucho who was called (because he had a bullet embedded in him) "El Chumbiao," surrounded the city of Paraná. One night, catching the garrison off guard, the rebels broke through the defenses and rode right around the central square, whooping like Indians and hurling insults. Then, still shouting and whistling, they galloped off. To them war was not a systematic plan of action but a manly sport.

The fourth of these stories, and my last, comes from the pages of an excellent book, *"L'Empire des Steppes* (1939), by the Orientalist René Grousset. Two passages from the second chapter are particularly relevant. Here is the first:

> Genghis Khan's war against the Chin, begun in 1211, was to last—with brief periods of truce—until his death (1227), only to be finished by his successor (1234). With their mobile cavalry, the Mongols could devastate the countryside and open settlements, but for a long time they knew nothing of the art of taking towns fortified by Chinese engineers. Be-

---

1. Burton writes that the Bedouins, in Arab cities, cover their nostrils with a handkerchief or stop them up with cotton wool; Ammianus, that the Huns avoided houses as people ordinarily avoid graves. So, too, with the Saxons, who invaded England and for a century dared not dwell in the Roman cities they conquered. They let them fall to ruin and composed elegies lamenting those ruins.

sides, they fought in China as on the steppe, in a series of raids, after which they withdrew with their booty, leaving the Chinese behind them to reoccupy their towns, rebuild the ruins, repair the breaches in the walls, and reconstruct the fortifications, so that in the course of that war the Mongol generals found themselves obliged to reconquer the same places two or three times.

Here is the second passage:

The Mongols took Peking, massacred the whole population, looted the houses, and then set fire to them. The devastation lasted a month. Clearly, the nomads had no idea what to do with a great city or how to use it for the consolidation and expansion of their power. We have here a highly interesting case for specialists in human geography: the predicament of the peoples of the steppe when, without a period of transition, chance hands them old countries with an urban civilization. They burn and kill not out of sadism but because they find themselves out of their element and simply know no better.

I now give a story that all the authorities agree upon. During Genghis Khan's last campaign, one of his generals remarked that his new Chinese subjects were of no use to him, since they were inept in war, and that, consequently, the wisest course was to exterminate them all, raze the cities, and turn the almost boundless Middle Kingdom into one enormous pasture for the Mongol horses. In this way, at least, use could be made of the land, since nothing else was of any value. The Khan was about to follow this counsel when another adviser pointed out to him that it would be more advantageous to levy taxes on the land and on goods. Civilization was saved, the Mongols grew old in the cities that they had once longed to destroy, and doubtless they ended up, in symmetrical gardens, appreciating the despised and peaceable arts of prosody and pottery.

Distant in time and space, the stories I have assembled are really one. The protagonist is eternal, and the wary ranch hand who spends three days behind a door that looks out into a backyard—although he has come down in life—is the same one who with two bows, a lasso made of horsehair, and a scimitar was poised to raze and obliterate the world's most ancient kingdom under the hooves of his steppe pony. There is a pleasure in detecting beneath the masks of time the eternal species of horseman and city.[2] This pleasure, in the case of these stories, may leave the Argentine with a melancholy aftertaste, since (through Hernández's gaucho Martín Fierro or through the weight of our past) we identify with the horseman, who in the end is the loser. The centaurs defeated by the Lapiths; the death of the shepherd Abel at the hand of Cain, who was a farmer; the defeat of Napoleon's cavalry by British infantry at Waterloo are all emblems and portents of such a destiny.

The horseman vanishing into the distance with a hint of defeat is, in our literature, the gaucho. And so we read in *Martín Fierro:*

*Cruz y Fierro de una estancia
una tropilla se arriaron;*

---

2. It is well known that the gauchesco poets Hildalgo, Ascasubi, Estanislao del Campo, and Lussich abounded in humorous anecdotes about the horseman's dialogue with the city.

por delante se la echaron
como criollos entendidos,
y pronto, sin ser sentidos,
por la frontera cruzaron.

Y cuando la habían pasao,
una madrugada clara,
le dijo Cruz que mirara
las últimas poblaciones;
y a Fierro dos lagrimones
le rodaron por la cara.

Y siguiendo el fiel del rumbo
se entraron en el desierto . . .

[From a ranch, Cruz and Fierro rounded up a herd of horses and, being practical gauchos, drove it before them. Undetected, they soon crossed over the border.

After this was done, early one morning Cruz told Fierro to look back on the last settlements. Two big tears rolled down Fierro's face.

Then, continuing on their course, the men set off into the wilderness . . .]

And in Lugones' *El Payador:*

In the fading twilight, turning brown as a dove's wing, we may have seen him vanish beyond the familiar hillocks, trotting on his horse, slowly, so that no one would think him afraid, under his gloomy hat and the poncho that hung from his shoulders in the limp folds of a flag at half mast.

And in *Don Segundo Sombra:*

> Still smaller now, my godfather's silhouette appeared on the slope. My eyes concentrated on that tiny movement on the sleepy plain. He was about to reach the crest of the trail and vanish. He grew less and less, as if he were being whittled away from below. My gaze clung to the black speck of his hat, trying to preserve that last trace of him.

In the texts just quoted, space stands for time and history.

The figure of the man on the horse is, secretly, poignant. Under Attila, the "Scourge of God," under Genghis Khan, and under Tamerlane the horseman tempestuously destroys and founds extensive empires, but all he destroys and founds is illusory. His work, like him, is ephemeral. From the farmer comes the word "culture" and from cities the word "civilization," but the horseman is a storm that fades away. In his book *Die Germanen der Völkerwanderung* (Stuttgart, 1939), Capelle remarks apropos of this that the Greeks, the Romans, and the Germans were agricultural peoples.

IX.
The Dagger

To Margarita Bunge

A dagger rests in a drawer.

It was forged in Toledo at the end of the last century. Luis Melián Lafinur gave it to my father, who brought it from Uruguay. Evaristo Carriego once held it in his hand.

Whoever lays eyes on it has to pick up the dagger and toy with it, as if he had always been on the lookout for it. The hand is quick to grip the waiting hilt, and the powerful obeying blade slides in and out of the sheath with a click.

This is not what the dagger wants.

It is more than a structure of metal; men conceived it and shaped it with a single end in mind. It is, in some eternal way, the dagger that last night knifed a man in Tacuarembó and the daggers that rained on Caesar. It wants to kill, it wants to shed sudden blood.

In a drawer of my writing table, among draft pages and old letters, the dagger dreams over and over its simple tiger's dream. On wielding it the hand comes alive because the metal comes alive, sensing itself, each time handled, in touch with the killer for whom it was forged.

At times I am sorry for it. Such power and single-mindedness, so impassive or innocent its pride, and the years slip by, unheeding.

X.
Foreword of an Edition
to the Complete Poems
of Evaristo Carriego

Nowadays we all see Evaristo Carriego in relation to the ragged outskirts of Buenos Aires, and we tend to forget that Carriego (like his neighborhood tough, his back-street seamstress, and his Italian immigrant) is a character out of Carriego, just as the Palermo in which we imagine him is a projection and almost an illusion of his work. Oscar Wilde held that Japan—that the images evoked by the word "Japan"—was the invention of Hokusai. In the case of Evaristo Carriego, may we not suggest a reciprocal process: the shabby suburb of Palermo creates Carriego and is re-created by him. The actual Palermo, the Palermo of Trejo's stage productions, and the milonga all influenced Carriego; Carriego puts over his view of Palermo; this view alters reality. (Later, reality will be altered still more by the tango and by popular theatrical pieces.)

How did it come to pass, how did that poor boy Carriego become what now he will be for all time? Carriego himself, if asked, perhaps could not tell us. With nothing more to recommend it than my inability to imagine things differently, I offer this explanation:

One day in 1904, in a house that still stands on Honduras Street, Evaristo Carriego regretfully and eagerly read the adventures of Charles de Baatz, lord of Artagnan. Eagerly, because Dumas offered Carriego what others are offered by Shakespeare or Balzac or Walt Whitman—a taste of the fullness of life. Regretfully, because Carriego was young, proud, shy, and poor, and he believed himself remote from life. Life was in France, he thought, in the sharp clash of steel or when Napoleon's armies were inundating the earth, but my lot has fallen to the twentieth century—the too late twentieth century—and a shabby South American suburb. Carriego was in the midst of this brooding reflection when something happened. The laborious tuning of a guitar, the uneven row of low houses seen from his window, Juan Muraña touching the brim of his hat in reply to a greeting (the same Muraña who two nights earlier had slashed the face of Suárez the Chilean), the moon from the square of a patio, an old man with a fighting cock—something, anything. Something we cannot pinpoint, something whose meaning we know but not its shape, something commonplace and hitherto unnoticed which revealed to Carriego that life (which offers itself wholly at every moment, anywhere, and not just in the works of Dumas) was there as well, in the despised present, in Palermo, in the year 1904. "Come in," said Heraclitus to those who found him warming himself in the kitchen, "the gods are here as well."

I have always suspected that any life, no matter how full or complex it may be, is made up essentially of a single moment—the moment in which a man finds out, once and for all, who he is. From the instant of that indeterminable revelation which I have tried to intuit, Carriego becomes Carriego. He is already the author of those verses which years later it will be allowed him to compose:

> Le cruzan el rostro, de estigmas violentos,
> hondas cicatrices, y quizás le halaga
> llevar imborrables adornos sangrientos:
> caprichos de hembra que tuvo la daga.

[Deep scars, violent stigmas, mark his face, and perhaps he is proud to wear ineradicable gory adornments: a knife's womanly capriciousness.]

In the last line, almost miraculously, is an echo of the medieval conceit of the marriage of the warrior with his weapon, of that conceit which Detlev von Liliencron captured in other famous lines:

> In die Friesen trug er sein Schwert Hilfnot,
> das hat ihn heute betrogen . . .

[He bore among the Frisians his sword Helpmeet, which today betrayed him . . .]

Buenos Aires
November 1950

XI.
A History of the Tango

Vicente Rossi, Carlos Vega, and Carlos Muzzio Sáenz Peña, painstaking researchers all, have each given a different version of the origins of the tango. I can state straightaway that I subscribe to every one of their conclusions—or, for that matter, to any other. From time to time films present us with their story of the development of the tango. According to this sentimental version, the tango seems to have been born on the outskirts of Buenos Aires, in tenements (in the Boca del Riachuelo, generally, by virtue of the photogenic qualities of that part of town). At the outset, the upper classes appear to have looked askance at the tango, but around 1910, under the tutelage of Paris, these same people seem finally to have thrown open their doors to this interesting product of the slums. This *Bildungsroman,* this tale of rags to riches, is by now a sort of incontestable or axiomatic truth. My memories (and I am over fifty) and the research into oral tradition that I have undertaken by no means confirm this.

I have spoken to José Saborido, who wrote the

tangos "Felicia" and "La morocha," to Ernesto Poncio, who wrote "Don Juan," to the brothers of Vicente Greco, who wrote "La viruta" and "La tablada," to Nicolás Paredes, the one-time political boss of Palermo, and to a few gaucho ballad singers of his acquaintance. Letting them speak, I carefully refrained from asking questions that led to expected answers. To my queries about the origin of the tango, I was given answers that differed widely as to locality and even country. Saborido, who was from Uruguay, favored Montevideo as the birthplace; Poncio, who was from Buenos Aires, opted for the Retiro, his own neighborhood; people from the Southside of Buenos Aires named Chile Street; people from the Northside, unsavory Temple Street or Junín Street.

Despite the differences I have listed, and which it would be easy to enrich by questioning people from other Argentine cities such as La Plata or Rosario, my informants agreed about one essential fact: that the tango originated in brothels. (The same was true of the date of that origin: none of them put it earlier than 1880 or later than 1890.) This testimony is confirmed by the cost of the instruments that tangos were first played on—the piano, flute, violin, and only later the concertina. It is proof that the tango did not arise in the city's shabby outskirts, where—as everyone knows—the six strings of a guitar had always been sufficient. There is no lack of further confirmation: the lasciviousness of the dance steps; the sexual connotations of certain titles ("El choclo" [The Corn Cob], "El fierrazo" [The Big Rod]); the fact, which as a boy I myself observed in Palermo and years later in Chacarita and Boedo, that it was danced on street corners by male couples, because decent women would have no part of such a wanton dance. Evaristo Carriego described this in his *Misas herejes:*

En la calle, la buena gente derrocha
sus guarangos decires más lisonjeros,
porque al compás de un tango, que es "La
    Morocha,"
lucen ágiles cortes dos orilleros.

[People in the street are lavish with vulgar approval, for to the rhythm of the tango "La morocha" two men from the outer slums are showing off suggestive dance steps.]

On another page, with a mass of poignant detail, Carriego describes a humble wedding celebration. The groom's brother is in jail; two young men are spoiling for a fight and the neighborhood tough has to use threats to keep the peace; there is suspicion, ill feeling, and horseplay, but

El tío de la novia, que se ha creído
obligado a fijarse si el baile toma
buen carácter, afirma, medio ofendido,
que no se admiten cortes, *ni aun en broma.*

—Que, la modestia a un lado, no se la pega
ninguno de esos vivos . . . seguramente.
La casa será pobre, nadie lo niega:
todo lo que se quiera, pero decente. —

[The bride's uncle, who has taken it upon himself to see that the dancing stays proper, states, somewhat shocked, that suggestive steps are not allowed—even in fun.

"For, modesty apart, not that any of these louts would know what I'm talking about, this house may be poor—there's no denying that—poor as anything, but respectable."]

This glimpse of the uncle's momentary strictness, which the two stanzas capture, is typical of people's first reaction to the tango—"that reptile from the brothel," as Lugones was to define it with laconic contempt (*El Payador*, page 117). It took a number of years for the Northside to introduce the tango—by then made respectable by Paris, of course—into its tenements, and I am not sure whether the introduction has been a complete success. What was once orgiastic devilry is now just another way of walking.

VIOLENCE AND THE TANGO

The tango's sexual nature has often been noted, but not so its violent side. Both, it is true, are modes or manifestations of the same impulse. In all the languages I know the word "manly" connotes sexual potentiality and a potential to bellicosity, and the word *virtus*, Latin for "courage," stems from *vir*, meaning "man." In the same way, an Afghan in the novel *Kim* can state—as if the two acts were essentially one—"When I was fifteen, I had shot my man and begot my man."

Merely to connect the tango with violence is not strong enough. I maintain that the tango and the milonga are a direct expression of something that poets have often tried to state in words: the belief that a fight may be a celebration. In Jordanes' sixth-century *History of the Goths,* we read that Attila, before his defeat at Châlons, addressed his armies, telling them that fortune had reserved for them "the joys of this battle" (*certaminis hujus gaudia*). The *Iliad* tells of the Achaeans, to whom war was sweeter than returning home in empty ships to their dearly loved native land, and relates how Paris, the son of Priam, ran swiftly to battle like a stallion that tosses its flowing mane in pursuit of mares. In the Old English epic Beowulf, the poet calls the battle a *"sweorda gelac,"* or "game of swords." Scandinavian skalds of the eleventh century called it "the festivity of Vikings." In the early part of the seventeenth century, Quevedo, in one of his *jácaras,* called a duel "a dance of swords," which is very near the anonymous Anglo-Saxon's "game of swords." In his evocation of the battle of Waterloo, Victor Hugo said that the soldiers, realizing that they were going to die in that festivity *("Comprenant qu'ils allaient mourir dans cette fête"),* stood erect amid the storm and hailed their god, the Emperor.

These examples, collected in the course of my random reading, could easily be multiplied. In the *Chanson de Roland,* perhaps, or in Ariosto's vast poem similar passages could be found. Some of those recorded here—the one by Quevedo or the one about Attila, let us say—are undeniably effective. All of them, however, suffer from the original sin of literariness: they are structures of words, constructs made up of symbols. "Dance of swords," for example, invites us to link two dissimilar things—the dance and combat—in order that the former infuse the latter with joy. But "dance of swords" does not speak directly to our blood; it does not re-create this joy in us. Schopenhauer (*Die Welt als Wille und Vorstellung,* I, 52) has written that music is altogether independent of the real world. Without the world, without a common stock of memories that can be evoked by language, there would certainly be no literature, but music stands in no need of the world; music could still exist even if there were no world at all. Music is will and passion; the old tango, as music, immediately transmits this joy of battle that Greek and Germanic poets tried long ago to express in words. A few present-day composers strive for this heroic tone and sometimes achieve it in milongas about the Batería or the Barrio del Alto, but their labors—their deliberately old-fashioned lyrics and music—are exercises in nostalgia for what once was, laments for what will never be again. Even when their melody is gay, these milongas remain basically sad. They are to the lusty, innocent ones recorded in Rossi's book what *Don Segundo Sombra* is to *Martín Fierro* or to *Paulino Lucero*.

We read in one of Oscar Wilde's conversations that music reveals to each of us a personal past which until then we were unaware of, moving us to lament misfortunes we never suffered and to feel guilt for acts we never committed. For myself, I confess that I cannot hear "El Marne" or "Don Juan" without remembering exactly an apocryphal past, at one and the same time stoic and orgiastic, in which I have thrown down the challenge and, in silence, met my end in an obscure knife fight. Perhaps this is the tango's mission: to give Argentines the conviction of having had a brave past, of having fulfilled the demands of bravery and honor.

THE CULT OF COURAGE

All over the Argentine runs a story that may belong to legend or to history or (which may be just another way of saying it belongs to legend) to both things at once, and that illustrates the cult of courage. Its best recorded versions are to be found in the unjustly forgotten novels about outlaws and desperadoes written in the last century by Eduardo Gutiérrez; among its oral versions, the first one I heard came from a neighborhood of Buenos Aires bounded by a penitentiary, a river, and a cemetery, and nicknamed Tierra del Fuego. The hero of this version was Juan Muraña, a wagon driver and knife fighter to whom are attributed all the stories of daring that still survive in what were once the outskirts of the city's Northside. That first version was quite simple. A man from the Stockyards or from Barracas, knowing about Muraña's reputation (but never having laid eyes on him), sets out all the way across town from the Southside to take him on. He picks the fight in a corner saloon, and the two move into the street to have it out. Each is wounded, but in the end Muraña slashes the other man's face and tells him, ''I'm letting you live so you'll come back looking for me again.''

What impressed itself in my mind about the duel was that it had no ulterior motive. In conversation thereafter (my friends know this only too well), I grew fond of retelling the anecdote. Around 1927 I wrote it down, giving it the deliberately laconic title ''Men Fought.'' Years later, this same anecdote helped me work out a lucky story—though hardly a good one—called ''Streetcorner Man.'' Then, in 1950, Adolfo Bioy-Casares and I made use of it again to plot a film script that the producers turned down and that would have been called *On the Outer Edge*. It was about hard-bitten men like Muraña who lived on the outskirts of Buenos Aires before the turn of the century. I thought, after such extensive labors, that I had said farewell to the story of the disinterested duel. Then, this year, out in Chivilcoy, I came across a far better version. I hope this is the true one, although since fate seems to take pleasure in a thing's happening many times over, both may very well be authentic. Two quite bad stories and a script that I still think of as good came out of the poorer first version; out of the second, which is complete and perfect, nothing can come. Without working in metaphors or details of local color, I shall tell it now as it was told to me. The story took place to the west, in the district of Chivilcoy, sometime back in the 1870s.

The hero's name is Wenceslao Suárez. He earns his wages braiding ropes and making harnesses, and lives in a small adobe hut. Forty or fifty years old, he's a man who has won a reputation for courage, and it is quite likely (given the facts of the story) that he has a killing or two to his credit. But these killings, because they were in fair fights, neither trouble his conscience nor tarnish his good name. One evening, something out of the ordinary happens in the routine life of this man: at a crossroads saloon, he is told that a letter has come for him. Don Wenceslao does not know how to read; the saloon keeper puzzles out word by word an epistle certainly not written by the man who sent it. In the name of certain friends, who value dexterity and true composure, an unknown correspondent sends his compliments to don Wenceslao, whose renown has crossed over the Arroyo del Medio into the Province of Santa Fe, and extends him the hospitality of his humble home in a town of the said province. Wenceslao Suárez dictates a reply to the saloon keeper. Thanking the other man for his expression of friendship, and explaining that he dare not leave his mother—who is well along in years—alone, he invites the other man to his own place in Chivilcoy, where a barbecue and a bottle or so of wine may be looked forward to. The months drag by, and one day a man riding a horse harnessed and saddled in a style unknown in the area inquires at the saloon for the way to Suárez's house. Suárez, who has come to the saloon to buy meat, overhears the question and tells the man who he is. The stranger reminds him of the letters they exchanged some time back. Suárez shows his pleasure that the other man has gone to the trouble of making the journey; then the two of them go off into a nearby field and Suárez prepares the barbecue. They eat and drink and talk at length. About what? I suspect about subjects involving blood and cruelty—but with each man on his guard, wary.

They have eaten, and the oppressive afternoon heat weighs over the land when the stranger invites don Wenceslao to join in a bit of harmless knife play. To say no would dishonor the host. They fence, and at first they only play at fighting, but it's not long before Wenceslao feels that the stranger is out to kill him. Realizing at last what lay behind the ceremonious letter, Wenceslao regrets having eaten and drunk so much. He knows he will tire before the other man, on whom he has a good nine or ten years. Out of scorn or politeness, the stranger offers him a short rest. Don Wenceslao agrees and, as soon as they take up their dueling again, he allows the other man to wound him on the left hand, in which he holds his rolled poncho.[1] The knife slices through his wrist, the hand dangles loose. Suárez, springing back, lays the bleeding hand on the ground, clamps it down under his boot, tears it off, feints a thrust at the amazed stranger's chest, then rips open his belly with a solid stab. So the story ends, except that, according to one teller, the man from Santa Fe is left lifeless, while to another (who withholds from him the dignity of death) he rides back to his own province. In this latter version, Suárez gives him first aid with the rum remaining from their lunch.

In this feat of Manco (One Hand) Wenceslao—as Suárez is now known to fame—certain touches of mildness or politeness (his trade as harness and rope maker, his qualms about leaving his mother alone, the exchange of flowery letters, the two men's leisurely conversation, the lunch) happily tone down and make the barbarous tale more effective. These touches lend it an epic and even chivalrous quality that we hardly find, for example—unless we have made up our minds to do so—in the drunken brawls of *Martín Fierro* or in the closely related but poorer story of Juan Muraña and the man from the Southside. A trait common to the two may, perhaps, be significant. In both of them, the challenger is de-

---

1. Montaigne (*Essays*, I, 49) says that this manner of fighting with cloak and dagger is very old, and quotes Caesar's finding, *"Sinistras sagis involvunt, gladiosque distringunt"*—"They wrapped their cloaks around their left arms and drew their swords" (*Civil War*, I, 75). Lugones, in *El Payador* (1916), quotes these verses from a sixteenth-century *romance* of Bernardo del Carpio:

   Revolviendo el manto al brazo,
   la espada fuera a sacar.

   [Wrapping the cape around his arm, he drew his sword.]

feated. This may be due to the mere and unfortunate necessity for the local champion to triumph, but also (and this is preferable) to a tacit disapproval of aggression, or (which would be best of all) to the dark and tragic suspicion that man is the worker of his own downfall, like Ulysses in Canto XXVI of the *Inferno*. Emerson, who praised in Plutarch's *Lives* "a Stoicism not of the schools but of the blood," would have liked this story.

What we have, then, is men who led extremely elementary lives, gauchos and others from along the banks of the River Plate and the Paraná, forging, without realizing it, a religion that had its mythology and its martyrs—the hard and blind religion of courage, of being ready to kill and to die. This cult is as old as the world, but it was rediscovered and lived in the American republics by herders, stockyard workers, drovers, outlaws, and pimps. Its music was in the *estilos,** the milongas, and the early tangos. I have said that this was an age-old cult. In a thirteenth-century saga, we read:

"Tell me, what do you believe in?" said the earl.
"I believe in my own strength," said Sigmund.

Wenceslao Suárez and his nameless antagonist, and many others whom myth has forgotten or has absorbed in these two, doubtless held this manly faith, and in all likelihood it was no mere form of vanity but rather an awareness that God may be found in any man.

A PARTIAL MYSTERY

Once we concede the tango's compensatory function, a small mystery remains. The independence of South America was, to a large extent, an Argentine affair. Men from the Argentine fought in battles all over the continent—in Maipú in Ayacucho, in Junín. Then came the civil wars, the war with Brazil, the uprisings against Rosas and Urquiza, the war with Paraguay, and the frontier wars with the Indians. Our military past is abundant; but the fact is that the Argentine, while he considers himself brave, identifies not with that past (in spite of the prominence given the study of history in our schools) but with the vast generic figures of the Gaucho and the Hoodlum. If I am not mistaken, this paradoxical idiosyncrasy can be explained. The Argentine finds his symbol in the gaucho, and not in the soldier, because the courage with which oral tradition invests the gaucho is not in the service of a cause but is pure. The gaucho and the hoodlum are looked upon as rebels; Argentines, in contrast to North Americans and nearly all Europeans, do not identify with the state. This may be accounted for by the generally accepted fact that the state is an unimaginable abstraction.[2] The truth is that the Argentine is an individual, not a citizen. To him, an aphorism like Hegel's "The State is the reality of an ethical Idea" seems a sinister joke. Films dreamed up in Hollywood repeatedly hold up to us the case of a man (usually a newspaper reporter) who befriends a criminal in order, ultimately, to turn him in to the

---

2. The state is impersonal; the Argentine thinks only in terms of personal relationships. For this reason, to him stealing public money is not a crime. I am stating a fact, not justifying or condoning it.

police. The Argentine, to whom friendship is a passion and the police a Mafia, feels that that "hero" is an incomprehensible scoundrel. He feels with Don Quixote that "each man should tend to his own sins" and that "an honest man should not go out of his way to be another man's jailer" (*Don Quixote*, I, 22). Often when faced with the empty symmetries of Spanish style, I thought that we differed hopelessly from Spain; these two quotations from *Don Quixote* were enough to convince me of my mistake. They are the quiet, secret sign of an affinity. One night in Argentine literature deeply confirms this—that night when a rural police sergeant called out that he would not be party to the crime of killing a brave man, and began fighting against his own men, shoulder to shoulder with the deserter Martín Fierro.

THE LYRICS

Uneven in quality, since, as everybody knows, they come from a thousand heterogenous pens, tango lyrics—whether the product of inspiration or industry—make up, after half a century, an almost inextricable *corpus poeticum,* which the historians of Argentine literature will read or at least defend. The popular, so long as people have stopped understanding it, so long as it has been aged by the years, manages to arouse the nostalgic veneration of scholars and gives rise to polemics and glossaries. It is not unlikely that by about 1990 the suspicion or the certainty may arise that the true poetry of our time will be found not in such Argentine classics as Banchs' *Urna* or Mastronardi's *Luz de provincia* but in the unpolished human pieces collected in a magazine like *El alma que canta,* which publishes hit songs. Guilty of negligence, I have neither bought nor studied this chaotic repository, but I am not unaware of its variety and the growing bounds of its subject matter. The first tangos had no lyrics, or, if they did, the lyrics were improvised and obscene. Some dealt with rustic life ("I am the loyal woman / of the Buenos Aires gaucho"), because their composers sought popular subjects, and low life and the slums were not poetic material—not then. Other tangos, like the related milonga,[3] were lighthearted bits of boasting ("When I tango I'm so sharp / that, turning a double whisk, / word reaches the Northside / if I am dancing on the South"). Later on, this genre, like certain French naturalistic novels or certain engravings by Hogarth, chronicled the seamy side of life ("Next you became the mistress / of an old pharmacist / and the police chief's son / cleaned you out"). After that came the deplorable conversion of down-and-out or rough neighborhoods to respectability ("Puente Alsina, / where have all your hooligans gone?" or "Where are those men and women, / the red neckerchiefs and tall-crowned hats that Requena used to know? / Where is my Villa Crespo of yesteryear? / The Jews moved in, and Triumvirato is no more"). From early on, the woes of secret or sen-

---

3.   *Yo soy del barrio del Alto,*
       soy del barrio del Retiro.
       Yo soy aquel que no miro
       con quien tengo que pelear,
       y a quien en milonguear,
       ninguno se puso a tiro.

[I come from the Barrio del Alto, I come from around the Retiro. I am a man who does not think twice about whom I have to fight, a man who can dance a milonga that nobody else can come near.]

timental love affairs kept many a pen busy ("Remember when you were with me / and you put on a
hat / and that leather belt / I pinched from another
tramp?"). Loneliness, as in the blues and in Spanish
literature, was a favorite theme ("The evening
was sad, / my darling, / when you abandoned me").
Tangos of recrimination, tangos of hatred, tangos
full of mockery or bitterness were written; today they
defy transcription or even memory. In some,
perhaps a bit more kindly, the revenge took the form
of a pardon and delighted in magnanimous gestures
("Just come in now that you are back / and don't be
afraid of the beating"). All the hustle and bustle of
the city began making its way into the tango; low life
and the slums were not its only subjects, and I can
remember pieces—was it back in the twenties?—that
were called "El Rosedal" (The Rose Garden) and
"Mis noches del Colón" (My Nights at the Opera).

At the opening of his satires, Juvenal wrote
memorably that everything which moved man—his
wishes, fears, wrath, pleasures of the flesh, intrigues,
joys—would be the subject of his book; with excus-
able license we could apply his famous *"quidquid
agunt homines"* to the sum of tango lyrics. We could
also say that they make up a vast random *comédie
humaine* of Buenos Aires life. At the end of the eighteenth century, the German philologist Wolf argued
that before it became an epic the *Iliad* was a series of
songs and rhapsodies; this, perhaps, leaves way for
the prophecy that—with time—tango lyrics will
make up a long civic poem or will suggest to some
ambitious person the writing of such a poem. Several
years ago, together with Silvina Bullrich, I compiled
a first anthology of the hoodlum. In the preface, I
wrote that

The hoodlum was the common man of the city and of its straggling outskirts, just as the gaucho was of the plains and hills. Venerated archetypes of the latter are Martín Fierro and Juan Moreira and Segundo Ramírez Sombra; of the former there is still no ineluctable symbol, although hundreds of tangos and popular theatrical pieces foreshadow one . . . . May this book serve as a stimulus to someone to write that hypothetical poem which will do for the hoodlum what *Martín Fierro* did for the gaucho. May that poem, like Hernández's, be less attentive to details than to the core of the matter, less accurate about speech and fashion than about the shape of a man's life.

It was Andrew Fletcher, the seventeenth-century Scottish political figure, who remarked that "if a man were permitted to make all the ballads, he need not care who should make the laws of a nation." This observation suggests that popular, or traditional, poetry can influence sentiments and shape behavior. If we apply this thesis to the Argentine tango, we would find in it a mirror of our daily lives and at the same time a mentor or model whose influence is certainly malignant. The early milonga and tango may have been foolish, even harebrained, but they were bold and gay. The later tango is like a resentful person who indulges in loud self-pity while shamelessly rejoicing at the misfortunes of others.

Back in 1926 I remember blaming the Italians (particularly the Genoese from the Boca) for the denigration of the tango. In this myth, or fantasy, of our "native" tango perverted by "gringos," I now see a clear symptom of certain nationalistic heresies that later swept the world—under the impetus of the Italians, of course. It was not the concertina, which some time ago I dubbed cowardly, or the busy songwriters of a seaside slum that made the tango what it is but the whole country. Besides, the old "natives" who fathered the tango were named Bevilacqua, Greco, or de Bassi.

There are those who may wish to object to my defamation of the present-day tango on the grounds that the transition from boldness or swagger to self-pity is not necessarily regrettable and may even be a sign of maturity. My imagined adversaries may go on to say that the simple, brash Ascasubi is to the doleful Hernández what the first tango is to the latest and that no one—except, perhaps, Jorge Luis Borges—ever dared infer from this lessening of joy that *Martín Fierro* is inferior to *Paulino Lucero*. The answer is easy. It is not just a question of the tango's hedonism but of its moral tone. In the everyday tango of Buenos Aires, in the tango of family reunions and respectable tearooms, there is a streak of vulgarity, an unwholesomeness of which the tango of the knife and the brothel never even dreamed.

Musically, the tango may not be important; its only importance is what we attribute to it. This is not unjust, but it applies equally to everything under the sun—to our own death, for example, or to the woman who rejects us. The tango can be argued about, and we do argue about it, but like all that is genuine it contains a secret. Dictionaries of music give a short, adequate definition, which meets with general approval. This definition is both elementary and straightforward, but a French or Spanish composer who—correctly following such a definition—pieces together a "tango" finds to his astonishment that he has constructed something that Argentine ears do not recognize, that our memories do not cherish, and that our bodies reject. It might be said that without Buenos Aires evenings and nights no tango can be made, and that the platonic idea of the tango—its form universal (that form which "La tablada" and "El choclo" barely spell out)—awaits us Argentines in heaven, and that this thriving species, however humble, has its place in the world.

XII.
Two Letters

The publication of one of the chapters of "A History of the Tango" brought the author the following letters, which now enrich this book:

Concepción del Uruguay
Entre Ríos
January 27, 1953

Mr. Jorge Luis Borges

I have read "The Challenge" ["The Cult of Courage"] in *La Nación* of December 28.

In view of the interest you have shown in deeds of the kind that you describe, I believe you will be pleased to hear a story which used to be told by my father, who died many years ago, and which he claimed he witnessed personally.

The place—the San José meat-salting plant in Puerto Ruiz, near Gualeguay, which was operated by the firm of Laurencena, Parachú, and Marcó.

The time—around the 1860s.

Among the personnel of the salting plant, who were almost all Basques, was a Negro named Fustel, whose fame for his skill with a knife had gone beyond the borders of the province, as you will see.

One day a rider arrived in Puerto Ruiz grandly dressed in the fashion of that day: a black woolen chiripa, fringed leggings, a silk handkerchief around his neck, a belt covered with silver coins; on a good horse smartly decked out: bit, breastband, stirrups, and bridle worked with silver and gold, and a matching knife.

He introduced himself, saying he came from the Fray Bentos salting plant, where he had heard about Fustel, and, considering himself fairly tough, he wanted a try against this other man.

It was easy to put the two in touch, and, there being no motive of any kind for ill-will, the duel was fixed for an appointed day and hour in that same place.

In the middle of a big circle formed by all the personnel of the salting plant and by others in the vicinity, the fight started and both men showed admirable skill.

After a long time, the Negro Fustel managed to reach his opponent's forehead with the tip of his knife, opening a wound which, although small, began to bleed a lot.

Seeing he was wounded, the stranger threw down his knife, and, extending a hand to his opponent, he said, "You're the better man, friend."

They became very good friends, and, on parting, they exchanged knives as a token of friendship.

It occurs to me that with your prestigious pen, this event, which I believe is true (my father never lied), might be useful to you in rewriting your film script, changing its title from "On the Outer Edge" to "A Gaucho's Chivalry" or something of the kind.

> Respectfully yours,
> [signed]
> Ernesto T. Marcó

> Chivilcoy
> Buenos Aires
> December 28, 1952

Mr. Jorge Luis Borges
c/o *La Nación*

Dear Sir:

Re: Comments on "The Challenge" (December 28, 1952).

My aim in writing this is not to correct but to provide information, inasmuch as only a few details of the incident differ, while the essential facts remain the same.

On frequent occasions I heard the story of the duel that serves as the basis for "The Challenge," appearing in today's *Nación*, from my father, who at the time lived on a farm he owned near Doña Hipólita's Saloon, in a field next to which the terrible duel took place between Wenceslao and the gaucho from Azul—the visitor himself told Wenceslao that he was from Azul, whither word of the former's reputation had reached—who had come to challenge the other's standing.

The two rivals ate beside a haystack, very likely sizing each other up, and when their spirits had risen the southerner extended an invitation to a bit of harmless knife play, which our man at once accepted.

Quick on his feet, the man from Azul kept out of reach of his rival's knife, prolonging the fight to Wenceslao's disadvantage. From the top of the haystack a man who worked for Doña Hipólita, who had closed up her saloon in view of the turn of events, fearfully witnessed the ups and downs of the fight. Determined to settle it one way or the other, Wenceslao lowered his guard, offering his left arm, which was protected by the poncho that was wrapped around it. The man from Azul struck like lightning with a terrific chopping blow that landed on his opponent's wrist just as the tip of Wenceslao's knife reached his eye. A wild scream rent the silence of the pampa, and the man from Azul took to his heels and sought refuge behind the heavy saloon door. Meanwhile, Wenceslao stepped on his left hand, which hung from a piece of skin, and with a single cut severed it from his arm, stuck the stump in the breast of his shirt, and ran after the fugitive, roaring like a lion and calling out for the other man to come out and finish the fight.

From that day on, Wenceslao was known as Manco (One Hand) Wenceslao. He lived off his trade as a harness and rope maker. He never started a fight. His presence in any saloon secured the peace, since his stern warning, spoken calmly in his manly voice, was enough to discourage anybody who was spoiling for a fight. In a poor place like that he was a gentleman. His humble life had meaning. His pride tolerated neither insult nor slight, and his deep knowledge of human weakness made him doubt the impartiality of the justice of that day, which is why he grew accustomed to dispensing justice himself.

Therein lay his error with regard to his own self-preservation.

A kick in the behind by an Italian obliged him to retaliate, and that was the start of his undoing. A large posse corraled him in a saloon where he had gone in search of vice. The knife fight, of 5 against 1, was going Wenceslao's way when a point-blank shot laid out forever the hero of the 13th precinct.

The rest of your account is accurate. He lived in a shack with his mother. The neighbors, among them my father, helped him build it. He never robbed.

May I take this opportunity to extend my heartfelt admiration to the talented author.

[signed]
Juan B. Lauhirat

Appendixes

Carriego and His Awareness of the City's Outskirts

On a street in Palermo whose name I *do* wish to recall—Honduras Street—there lived during the important Centenary years a consumptive Entrerriano, almost a genius, who observed the neighborhood with an immortalizing look. That Palermo of
yesterday was somewhat different from the Palermo
of today. There were hardly any two-story houses
then, and behind the brick-paved entranceways and
the even line of rooftop balustrades the patios were
brimming with sky, with grapevines, and with girls.
There were vacant lots that welcomed the sky, and in
the evenings the moon seemed more alone, and light
together with an odor of strong rum emanated from
the back rooms of shops. In that yesterday the neighborhood was violent; it took pride in the fact that it
was called Tierra del Fuego, and the legendary crimson of Palermo de San Benito still lived in the knives
of unsavory characters. There were hoodlums in

those days, foul-mouthed men who passed the time behind a whistle or a cigarette and whose distinctive features were a thick head of hair worn swept back, a silk neckerchief, high-heeled boots, a swaggering walk, and an aggressive stare. It was the classic era of street-corner gangs and troublemakers. Bravery, or a pretense of bravery, was in the air, and Ño Moreira (who hailed from Matanzas, on the western outskirts of the city, and was elevated by Eduardo Gutiérrez to semidivinity) was still the champ Luis Ángel Firpo, whom the louts idolized. Evaristo Carriego, the Entrerriano I mentioned at the beginning of this piece, observed these things for all time and gave voice to them in poems that are the soul of the Argentine soul.

So true is this that the words "outskirts" and "Carriego" are today synonyms of a single vision—one brought to perfection by death and veneration, since the demise of the person who gave rise to that vision gives him poignancy at the same time as it links his vision indissolubly to the past. His modest twenty-nine years and his early death lend prestige to that shabby setting which was the background of his work. He himself has been invested with a tameness, and so in José Gabriel's mythifying there is a pusillanimous and almost effeminate Carriego who is certainly not the man with the stinging tongue and the endless talker that I knew in my boyhood on his Sunday visits to my home.

His poems have been judged by everyone. Nevertheless, I want to point out that, in spite of a good deal of obvious and clumsy sentimentality, they have touches of tenderness, glimpses and perceptions of tenderness, as true as this one:

Y cuando no estén, ¿durante
cuánto tiempo aún se oirá
su voz querida en la casa
desierta?
        ¿Como serán
en el recuerdo las caras
que ya no veremos más?

[And when they are gone, how much longer will
their dear voices be heard in the empty house? How
will their faces, which we will no longer see, look in
our memory?]

I want also to give wholehearted praise to his
characterization of the organ grinder, in a piece
which Oyuela considers his best and which in my
opinion is perfect.

        El ciego te espera
las más de las noches sentado
a la puerta. Calla y escucha. Borrosas
memorias de cosas lejanas
evoca en silencio, de cosas
de cuando sus ojos tenían mañanas
de cuando era joven . . . la novia . . . ¡quién sabe!

[The blind man waits for you, seated most nights by
his door. In silence, he recalls faded memories of distant things, things when his eyes beheld the morning, when he was young, his girl, who knows what!]

The soul of these lines is not in the final verse; it
is in the next to last, and I suspect that Carriego put
it there so as not to lay emphasis on it. In another,
earlier poem called "El alma del suburbio," he had

already sketched the same subject, and it is worth comparing that first treatment (a realistic picture made up of minute observations) with the later serious, compassionate festivity in which he gathers the favorite symbols of his art—the back-street seamstress who came to grief, the moon, and the blind man.

They are melancholy symbols all, depressing and cheerless. It is the custom today to suppose that apathy and loud self-pity are the hallmarks of those who live on the city's outskirts. I think otherwise. A tug or two of the concertina fail to convince me, as do the vulgar woes of mawkish petty criminals or more or less repentant prostitutes. The present-day tango, concocted of picturesqueness and labored *lunfardo* jargon, is one thing; and the old tangos, made of blatant impudence, shamelessness, and joyous courage, are another. They were the hoodlum's true voice; the latter tangos (both music and lyrics) are the invention of those who disbelieve in the hoodlum's bravery, of those who explain and set you right about it. The first tangos—"El caburé," "El cuzquito," "El flete," "El apache argentino," "Una noche de garufa," and "Hotel Victoria"—still testify to the rollicking courage of the outer slums. Words and music went together. Of the tango "Don Juan," about the neighborhood tough, I recall these boastful bad lines:

> *En el tango soy tan taura*
> *que cuando hago un doble corte*
> *corre la voz por el Norte*
> *si es que me encuentro en el Sur.*

[When I tango I'm so sharp that, turning a double

whisk, word reaches the Northside if I'm dancing on the South.]

But all that is old, and in the outer slums today we are only out for misfortune. Obviously, Carriego is somewhat responsible for our gloomy impressions. More than anyone, he has dulled the bright colors of the city's outer edge; he holds the innocent blame for the fact that, in the tango now, the wenches one and all go to the hospital and the hoodlums are ruined by morphine. In this sense, his work is the antithesis of that of Álvarez, who was an Entrerriano and, like Carriego, made himself into a man of Buenos Aires. We must confess, however, that Álvarez's vision has little or no lyric importance, while Carriego's is captivating. He has filled our eyes with compassion, and it is obvious that compassion needs faults and weaknesses so that it can console itself afterward. This is why we must forgive him that none of the girls in his book get betrothed. If he arranged it that way, it was in order to love them better and to expose their hearts, made pitiful by sorrow.

This all-too-brief discourse on Carriego has another side, and I must return to the subject one day simply to praise him. I suspect that Carriego is now in heaven (in some Palermitano heaven, doubtless the same one to which the old city gates were taken) and that the Jew Heinrich Heine will have paid him a visit and by now the two will be close friends.

Foreword to an Edition
of the Selected Poems of
Evaristo Carriego

Two cities, Paraná and Buenos Aires, and two dates, 1883 and 1912, define in time and space the short span of Evaristo Carriego's life. Directly descended from old Entre Ríos stock and feeling a nostalgia for the brave past of his forebears, he sought a kind of compensation in the romantic novels of Dumas, in the legend of Napoleon, and in the idolatrous worship of the gaucho. In this way, partly *pour épater les bourgeois,* partly under the spell of the Podestá brothers and of Eduardo Gutiérrez, he dedicated one of his poems to the memory of San Juan Moreira.[1] The details of Carriego's life can be summed up in a few words. He worked on a newspaper, he mixed in literary circles, and, like his whole generation, he got drunk on Almafuerte, Darío, and Jaimes Freyre. As a boy, I heard Carriego recite from memory the 150-

---

1. *Martín Fierro* had not yet been canonized by Leopoldo Lugones.

odd stanzas of Almafuerte's *Misionero,* and after all these years I can still hear the passion in his voice. I know little of his political opinions; it is not unlikely that he was vaguely and loftily an anarchist. Like all cultured South Americans of the beginning of the century, he was—or he felt he was—a sort of honorary Frenchman, and around 1911 he set out to acquire a first-hand knowledge of the language of Hugo, another of his idols. Carriego read and reread *Don Quixote,* and it is perhaps indicative of his taste that he preferred Herrera y Reissig to Lugones. The names so far listed may well exhaust the catalog of his modest but not negligible reading. He wrote continuously, driven by the sweet fever of tuberculosis. Aside from a few pilgrimages to Almafuerte's house in La Plata, he made no other journeys than those that history and historical novels can bestow on a mind. He died at twenty-nine, at the same age and of the same illness as John Keats.* Both hungered after fame, a legitimate passion at that time, which was still a stranger to the evil arts of publicity.

Esteban Echeverría was the first observer of the Argentine pampa; similarly, Carriego was the first observer of the outskirts of Buenos Aires. He could not have done his work without the wide freedom of vocabulary, subject matter, and metrics that modernism bestowed on the literatures of the Spanish language, on this or the other side of the ocean, but the modernism that inspired him also harmed him. A good half of *Misas herejes* is made up of unconscious parodies of Darío and Herrera. Despite these poems and the sundry defects of the rest, the discovery—let us call it that—of the literary possibilities of the run-down and ragged outskirts of Buenos Aires is Carriego's main significance.

To do this work really well, it would have been better had Carriego been either a man of letters, sensitive to the shades of meaning or to the connotations of words, or an uneducated man who was closer to the humble characters from whom he drew his subject matter. Unfortunately, he was neither. Bits of his reading of Dumas and the luxuriant vocabulary of modernism came between him and Palermo, and so it was inevitable that he would compare his knife fighter with D'Artagnan. In two or three pieces from *El alma del suburbio* he touched on the epic and in others, on social protest; in the poems of "La canción del barrio" he went from the "cosmic holy rabble" to the respectable middle class. His most famous if not his best pieces belong to this second and final stage. It was by this path that he arrived at what it would not be unjust to call the poetry of everyday misfortunes; of sickness; of disappointments; of time, which wears us down and crushes our spirit; of family life; of tenderness; of habit; and almost of gossip. It is interesting that the tango followed the same evolution.

In Carriego, we can see the fate of the forerunner. Work that seemed unusual to his contemporaries today runs the risk of appearing trivial. Fifty years after his death, Carriego belongs less to poetry than to the history of poetry.

His was the early death that seems part of the destiny of a romantic poet. I have asked myself more than once what he would have written if he had lived longer. One exceptional poem, "El casamiento," may foreshadow a turn toward humor. This, of course, is a guess; what is undeniable is that Carriego influenced—and goes on influencing—the course of Argentine literature and that some of his poems will become part of that anthology toward which all writing aspires. To the characters in his work—the local tough, the seamstress who got into trouble, the blind man, and the organ grinder—we must add another, the consumptive youth, dressed in black, who used to saunter among the single-story houses of Palermo, trying out a line or stopping now and again to look at something he was soon to leave behind.

Postscript, 1974—Poetry works with the past. The Palermo of *Misas herejes* was that of Carriego's boyhood, and I never knew that Palermo. Poetry demands the nostalgia, the patina—albeit slight—of time. We see this process in gauchesco literature as well. Ricardo Güiraldes celebrated what once existed, what might have existed—his Don Segundo— not what existed at the time he wrote his elegy.

Notes

Page 7.   *The dedication.* This was added in the second edition.

Page 9.   *The epigraph.* It is given here exactly as it appears in De Quincey. Borges, however, has quoted it as "a mode of truth, not of truth coherent and central, but angular and splintered."

Page 39.   *Juan Manuel de Rosas.* After six years (1810–16) of fruitless military effort to incorporate the outlying provinces of the old Viceroyalty of the Río de la Plata—Uruguay, Paraguay, and Bolivia—the provinces of modern-day Argentina determined to declare their own independence from Spain. But as the jealousies and antagonisms deepened between liberal Buenos Aires intellectuals and the people of the interior, the search for a viable form of government became more and more elusive. The delegates of the 1816 Tucumán Congress, who signed the independence act, appointed an interim supreme dictator while they went about looking for a king. The supreme dictator ruled until 1819. Meanwhile, the power of local bosses, the caudillos, who held sway over their bands of gaucho cavalry (*montoneras*), had so increased that it soon became apparent that they would oppose king, dictator, or president. When, in 1819, Congress drafted a highly centralist constitution, the provincial caudillos opposed it. The next fifteen years were fraught with disunity, chaos, and civil war. In this period, the two great factions rose: the Unitarians (*unitarios*), who favored a centralist government under Buenos Aires leadership; and the Federalists (*federales*), who demanded local autonomy and at the same time recognition by Buenos Aires of their rights in the national partnership. While the Unitarians, who included a large part of the wealthy and cultured families of Buenos Aires, were clear in their stand, the Federalists were split between mutually suspicious provincial caudillos and the Buenos Aires party. Federalism, for each of these factions, proved to hold different meanings, and by the end of Rosas's reign it was little more than a cover for the self-serving sectionalism of the capital and the ranchers of Buenos Aires province.

Out of this upheaval of the 1820s, in the search for a man strong enough to crush all opposition, came Juan Manuel de Rosas. Born in 1793 to a leading Buenos Aires family, he grew up on the pampa on his father's ranch, of which he became manager at the age of sixteen. Competent, strict but just with his gauchos, by the age of twenty-five Rosas was a large landowner and cattle breeder, and by 1820 a powerful caudillo. With his small army, dressed by him in red (which became the color of the Federalists), he began intervening in politics; in 1829, he marched on Buenos Aires to put down an uprising, and in the outcome he was installed as governor. As a result of intense political intrigue, Rosas had become the chosen instrument of a powerful group of landowners in the Province of Buenos Aires who were convinced that their well-being would be ensured if control of the province and domination of the nation's major port were vested in their own number. Rosas's immediate policy was the punishment of his enemies and the demand of total submission to the Federalist party. The purge of Unitarian army chiefs began; some were shot, others jailed, and the display of red ribbons on all persons became obligatory. His term up in 1832, Rosas refused re-election when the legislature would not extend his dictatorial powers, and for the next three years he dedicated himself to extending the borders of the province into Indian territory to the south and west of Buenos Aires. During this expedition, 6,000 hostiles were killed. Meanwhile, in the capital, Rosas's wife (according to certain sources) worked hard for his return; in an effort to stage an uprising, she founded a terrorist organization known as the *mazorca.*

Three weak governors floundered in power, until at last the legislative council begged Rosas to return. He did—on his own terms: "total power . . . for as long as he thinks necessary." Installed again in 1835, for the next seventeen years Rosas ruled the country with an iron hand. The terror spread, and the dictator was proclaimed "Restorer of the Laws." In the streets, the watchmen called out the hours with the chant, "Long live the Federation! Death to the savage Unitarians!" This was repeated in the press, from the pulpit, and in the schools. Of this terror, an American resident reported: "I have seen guards at mid-day enter the houses of citizens and either destroy or bear off the furniture . . . , turning the families into the streets, and committing other acts of violence too horrible to mention." In the marketplace, he continued, "Rosas hung the bodies of his many victims; sometimes decorating them in mockery, with ribands of the Unitarian blue and even attaching to the corpses, labels, on which were inscribed the revolting words 'Beef with the hide.'" Ironically, though Rosas never took a grander title than Governor of Buenos Aires, his rule was far more centralist than the Unitarians had ever dreamed. In his foreign policy, Rosas engaged the country in a war with Bolivia (1837–39); intervened in the affairs of Uruguay throughout the 1830s and 1840s; got himself into a costly war with France (1838–40); and suffered a blockade at the hands of an Anglo-French force (1845–48). Finally, by 1852, he had lost his support. A rival caudillo, Justo José de Urquiza, with Brazilian and Uruguayan aid, marched upon Buenos Aires and defeated Rosas's Federalists at Monte Caseros on February 3. Resigning as governor, the dictator fled and was carried into exile aboard a British warship. He settled on a small farm in Southhampton, where he died in 1877; his remains have never been repatriated.—Reprinted, with changes, from *Selected Poems* by Jorge Luis Borges, ed. Norman Thomas di Giovanni (New York: Delacorte Press/Seymour Lawrence, 1972), pp. 289–90, by permission of the author.

Page 43.   *Milonga.* The milonga is a forerunner of the tango dating from the 1890s. Possibly it was invented as a parody of Negro dances. As a musical composition it is lively and bold. It is the form used by improvisors (*payadores*) in their singing contests and the form which has inspired Borges to write numerous lyrics. The first milongas were danced.

Page 54.   *Servants in a forest of feather dusters.* Reference to the fact that the Spaniard performed menial tasks, working as domestic servants, cleaners, waiters, and so forth.

Page 59.   *Sáenz Peña Act.* Election reform laws that included honest registration of voters, compulsory voting, the use of secret ballots, and so on. It served, among other things, to bring large numbers of voters to the polls.

Page 77.   *Gato.* Quick and lively, the *gato* is an old Argentine dance that was very popular in the last century.

Page 78.   *Alsina.* Adolfo Alsina (1829–77) was an ardent partisan of autonomy for the Province of Buenos Aires, of which he was made governor in 1866; he also served as vice-president of the Republic in 1868.

Page 86.   *Another Salaverría.* The reference is to Unamuno.

Page 117.   *A smutty milonga.* The words Borges has in mind are *"Escaparás de mis bolas, pero de mi pija, cuándo."* (You may escape from my balls, but from my prick—never.)

Page 141.   *Estilo.* Usually played on the guitar, the *estilo* is a characteristic musical composition of the River Plate region. One of its favored subjects is love. It is rhythmically slow and somewhat emotional in nature.

Page 162.   *John Keats.* In fact, Keats (1795–1821) was twenty-six when he died.

Bibliographical Note

Certain of the parts of this volume made their first appearances in Spanish in the following newspapers or magazines (place of publication, throughout, unless otherwise indicated, is Buenos Aires):

CHAPTER VI

[CARRIEGO'S VERSES]: "Día de bronca" (signed with the pseudonym "El Barretero"), *L[adrón]. C[onocido]*. (September 26, 1912).

TRUCO: "El truco," *La Prensa* (January 1, 1928).

CHAPTER VII

INSCRIPTIONS ON WAGONS: "Las inscripciones de carro" (entitled "Séneca en las orillas"), *Síntesis* (December 1928).

CHAPTER VIII

STORIES OF HORSEMEN: "Historias de jinetes," *Comentario* (January–February–March 1954).

CHAPTER IX

THE DAGGER: "El puñal," *Marcha* (Montevideo, June 25, 1954).

CHAPTER XI

THE CULT OF COURAGE: "El culto del coraje" (in a somewhat different form and entitled "El desafío" [The Challenge]), *La Nación* (December 28, 1952).

APPENDIX I

CARRIEGO AND HIS AWARENESS OF THE CITY'S OUTSKIRTS: "Carriego y el sentido del arrabal," *La Prensa* (April 4, 1926).

"El truco" was first collected in *El idioma de los argentinos* (M. Gleizer, 1928); the rest of chapters I–VII, in the first edition of *Evaristo Carriego* (M. Gleizer, 1930). Printing of this first edition was completed on September 30, 1930.

Chapter X, the "Foreward to an Edition of the Complete Poems of Evaristo Carriego" ("Prólogo a una edición de las poesías completas de Evaristo Carriego"), first served as an introduction to Carriego's *Poesías* (Renacimiento, 1950) and was previously collected in *Otras inquisiciones* 1937–1952 under the title "Nota sobre Carriego" (A Footnote on Carriego). The rest of chapters VIII–XII were first collected in the second edition of *Evaristo Carriego* (Emecé, 1955).

''Carriego y el sentido del arrabal'' was first collected in *El tamaño de mi esperanza* (Proa, 1926).

The ''Foreword to an Edition of the Selected Poems of Evaristo Carriego'' first served as an introduction to *Versos de Carriego* (Eudeba, 1963); it has also been collected in *Prólogos; con un prólogo de prólogos (Torres Agüero,* 1975).